MITZ

THE MARMOSET OF BLOOMSBURY

MITZ

Sigrid Nunez

HarperFlamingo

An Imprint of HarperCollins*Publishers*

FIRST EDITION

Designed by Elina D. Nudelman

Library of Congress Cataloging-in-Publication Data

Nunez, Sigrid.
 Mitz : the marmoset of Bloomsbury / Sigrid Nunez. — 1st ed.
  p. cm.
 ISBN 0-06-017407-2
 1. Mitz (Monkey)—Fiction. 2. Woolf, Virginia, 1882–1941—Fiction.
3. Bloomsbury (London, England)—History—Fiction. 4. Marmosets—Fiction. 5. Woolf, Leonard, 1880–1969—Fiction. I. Title.
PS3564.U475M57 1998
813'.54—dc21   97-37626

98 99 00 01 02 ❖/RRD 10 9 8 7 6 5 4 3 2 1

At that time I had a marmoset called Mitz which accompanied me almost everywhere, sitting on my shoulder or inside my waistcoat.

—LEONARD WOOLF, *Downhill All the Way*

MITZ

I

It was a Thursday in July. That afternoon Leonard and Virginia Woolf drove from London to Cambridge to visit their young friends Barbara and Victor Rothschild. The Rothschilds had been married the December before. They lived in a grand old gray house called Merton Hall. When the Woolfs arrived, they found Barbara waiting outside for them. She sat on a chair on the lawn, a large straw hat shading her pretty face. They had known her since she was a baby. Now here she was expecting a baby herself.

They had tea—just the three of them; Victor was napping. Fresh lemonade—with gin, if they liked—and thin, freshly cut sandwiches. The room was filled with flowers set in large alabaster bowls. A bee had got indoors and kept drifting from bowl to bowl, from red rose to yellow rose, murmuring indecisively. Barbara was indecisive too. What to name the child if a boy? What to name the child if a girl? She and Victor were going abroad soon—where should they stay? Then Victor joined them, ruddy and bright-eyed from his nap and all eager to show them the garden. Virginia, who was very particular about gardens, did not like this one ("stuck like a jam tart . . . a pretentious uncared for garden," she derided it two days later in her diary).

As they strolled the narrow paths—Virginia with Victor; Barbara and Leonard behind them—the afternoon shaded to evening. It had been a scorching day. Now came a breeze, pleasantly moist, and a nightingale sang. The sun, suspended between two dark elms, quivered like a struck gong. It would have been a shame to go in, and so they ate dinner on the lawn, with the shadows darkening and the sky turning ever different, deeper blues. When the first stars appeared, the nightingale fell silent, as if this were what it had been singing for.

It was a sumptuous dinner. Leonard ate with delight, praising the fish, the meat, and the wine. But though she admired the lavishness with which they were being regaled, Virginia ate slowly, without appetite. This was not unusual; Virginia often had to force herself to eat. But when Leonard praised the fish, Virginia praised it too. When he said his chop was perfectly done, she said that hers was too. And when he took a sip of his wine and pronounced it superb, she nodded agreement, though she had not yet taken a sip of her own. Much care had been taken to please them, and such care must be thanked.

Though she shared in the conversation and heard every word, Virginia never stopped taking in what was happening around them. A writer, said her father's old friend Henry James, must be someone who notices everything. (So avidly did Virginia observe this rule, Leonard sometimes had to chide her in public for staring.) The changing light, the changing colors of the sky, the flight of swallow and bat, when the nightingale sang and when it did not—none of this was missed by Virginia. They were eating dessert—strawberries and cream—when she noticed something across the lawn. Some creature, small and gray. But what? Virginia narrowed her eyes and tried to discern it. A squirrel, she thought. But no: it was about the size of a squirrel, but it did not move like one. This thing crept, Virginia observed, as squirrels do not. No, that was not the brisk, skip-hopping scuttle of the squirrel. Was it a rat? she wondered, noticing now, with a slight shudder, the long thin tail. Again no. That was not the unmistakable hunched silhouette of the rat. Could it be a cat, then? A very small cat—a kitten? Virginia remembered that she had seen a cat earlier, when they were having tea, and she had counted four kittens tumbling about the garden. But none of them, as she recalled, had been gray.

It was not a kitten. It was—

"A marmoset."

Victor said the words just as Virginia was about to say them herself. Among the many pets that had lived at one time or another at her childhood home in Kensington there had been a marmoset. But that had been very long ago, and Virginia had all but forgotten it.

Now Victor picked up his plate and laid it on the ground. He clicked his tongue. "Mitz!" he called. "Here, Mitz! Come, come!" And Mitz came—not bounding across the lawn as might have been expected, but slowly, haltingly, like a toy dragged by a string.

"I'm afraid she's not very healthy," Victor said. "I think she's got rickets."

How small she was! A mere scrap of monkey. You could have balanced her on your palm, like a fur apple. A head no bigger than a walnut, two black pips for eyes, and the tiniest nostrils—mere pinpricks. Her fur was mostly gray—squirrel gray—but tufts of lighter fur grew out from the sides and the back of her head (a rather clownish effect, it must be said). Seizing a strawberry in both paws, she crammed it into her mouth. She ate far too quickly to enjoy it, with quick glances left and right, as if she feared some other creature would appear out of the grass to snatch it from her. Now she had cream all over her face. Still chewing, she picked up another berry and began to cram it into her mouth. While the others laughed, Virginia looked away. Virginia was squeamish about gluttony. ("I dont like greed when it comes to champing & chawing & sweeping up gravy," she once told her diary, raging against a certain dinner guest.) But Virginia was too fascinated to avert her eyes for long. Something human, all too human, about that naked little face—Virginia had always imagined the faces of elves looking perhaps like this. Elfin face, body and tail of a rodent: it was this combination that made Mitz such a wonder. You looked at her and thought, How grotesque. And the very next instant, How adorable. And then, How grotesque, again.

"Where did she come from?" Leonard asked.

"South America, originally," said Victor. "I found her in a junk shop. I bought her for Barbara." At this Barbara said nothing, but the way she rolled her eyes spoke loudly enough. Virginia understood. A healthy monkey was a strange enough gift for a woman expecting a baby. A *sickly* one . . .

"Funny thing about this species," said Victor, perhaps

also reminded at that moment of his wife's condition. "The males help the females to give birth."

Virginia's jaw dropped. An astonishing picture rose in her mind. "How—what—?"

"*We* don't think *we* want to know," said Barbara, rolling her eyes again and gently patting her domed midriff (the child was due in September).

A footman arrived to clear the table. Glancing at Leonard, Virginia saw that he was frowning, and she thought she knew exactly what his thoughts were: A junk shop! What had this poor creature been doing in a junk shop? Victor was right: Mitz was not healthy. That halting walk probably did mean rickets. Her coat was not sleek as it should have been, but rough- and dry-looking, with a few bald pink spots where sores might have healed. The fur round her neck was worn away and the skin was chafed. Apparently, Mitz had once been chained. . . .

Berries devoured, every last trace of cream licked away, Mitz uttered a string of cries—a shrill, gibbering monkey-sentence that rose at the end, like a question. As no one could interpret, no one could answer. She searched the four faces hovering against the darkening sky, and whatever it was she wanted she seemed to find in Leonard's long thin bony one. She jumped in his lap.

"You've made a friend," said Barbara. And Victor said, "I've never seen her take so quickly to anyone."

Virginia was not surprised. The Woolfs (or the Woolves as they were more commonly known) had been married for twenty-two years, and in twenty-two years Virginia had had many occasions to witness how animals took to her husband. He was a great lover of animals, and if he had found a sick monkey languishing in a junk shop she was sure he would have rescued it just as Victor had done.

Though she was also sure he would never have tried to pass it off as a gift.

Mitz perched on Leonard's knee. With the tip of one finger, he was rubbing the top of her head in a circular motion, in a way she seemed to like. Her eyes closed. She wrapped her tail tightly around her. She dozed.

Brandy was served. Leonard lit his pipe and Victor his cigar. Conversation resumed. Conversation was mostly serious that night and kept coming round—as was no doubt the case at many another dinner table—to the same topic. Three weeks earlier, in Germany, hundreds of people had been slaughtered. This had confirmed many people's worst fears about Hitler, who had come to power the year before. These days the possibility of war was on everyone's mind. For the Woolfs the 1914 war remained a searing memory. One of Leonard's brothers had been killed in that war and another badly wounded (in the same attack, as it happened, and hit by the very same shell). Another war such as the 1914 war and, Leonard said, civilization would be destroyed.

The breeze that had cooled them while they ate had turned sharper. Barbara snuggled deeper into her shawl. Virginia draped a cardigan over her shoulders. Within the house, servants were going from room to room, closing windows, drawing curtains. Mitz smacked her lips in her sleep—dreaming of berries and cream?

Leonard looked at his watch. "Good heavens," he said. It was past ten. The Woolfs had to be going. Leonard stood up, waking Mitz, and as he tried to put her down, she clung to his sleeve, his trouser leg, his shoe.

"I believe she's fallen in love," Victor said, and everyone laughed.

Before the Woolfs drove home, they were taken back

into the house to see the library. Victor had a very fine collection of books, many rare editions, encased in red morocco. The Woolfs admired a volume of Wordsworth, a first edition of *Gulliver's Travels*. Most of the books had been bought recently—it was Virginia's *The Common Reader* that had awakened the bibliophile in him, Victor said. Again Virginia bit her tongue, saving her criticism for her diary: "Ah but this isnt the way to read. . . . Too easy; sitting at Sotheby's bidding."

On the way back to London Virginia kept yawning. They did not usually stay out so late. She and Leonard talked about the evening, poking fun at their friends (the garden, the books), just as rich people so often fear literary people whom they've wined and dined will do on their way home. Still, there was much to be envied about the Rothschilds. Not the wealth, for the Woolfs disdained wealth, but the future, the baby coming in September, their whole lives ahead of them. In a word: youth.

Twenty-two years before, when they were first married, Leonard and Virginia had thought they too would have children.

They drove with the top cranked back. The road was empty, the fields were black. It was midnight, the nineteenth of July, 1934.

2

The Woolfs lived at 52 Tavistock Square. The house, which had been their home for ten years, had four floors. Leonard and Virginia lived on the second and third floors; the ground and first floors were let to the firm of Dollmann & Pritchard, solicitors. In the basement was an old billiard room that Virginia had taken over for her studio. There, amid a disorder that never ceased to amaze her husband, she could be found of a morning, sunk in a big old tattered armchair with a plywood board across her knees, dipping her pen into the inkpot that she had glued to the board, writing.

In the basement was also where the Woolfs had their press. The Hogarth Press, which the Woolfs had begun in 1917 (having agreed that nothing could be more fun for a writer than to publish his or her own books), had grown with the years into an important business. The Woolfs published some of the best writers of their day, and they published their friends (sometimes but not always the same people).

The Woolfs had a routine that seldom varied. Every morning at about nine-thirty, right after breakfast (which Leonard always served Virginia in bed), they went to their separate rooms to write. They wrote from nine-thirty until one. The Woolfs had spent so many mornings of their lives in this way that by 1934 they had written more than a score of books between them. At one, they joined each other for lunch. Sometimes there would be a guest. It might be Virginia's sister, Vanessa Bell, or one of Vanessa's children; or it might be one of the Woolfs' many friends: Maynard Keynes, or E. M. Forster, who was called Morgan, or Tom Eliot, or Vita Sackville-West. Often these days (too often, Virginia complained) it was garrulous Ethel Smyth, whose visits always left Virginia worn out and hoarse, partly from shouting into Ethel's ear trumpet.

After lunch the Woolfs would read their mail and the newspapers. Afternoons were usually devoted to typing out and revising that morning's work or taking care of business related to the Press. When the weather was fine (and often even when it was not), Virginia liked to include a long walk in her afternoon schedule. Walking was one of her deepest passions. She had inherited this passion, along with her passion for literature, from her father, Leslie Stephen, a famous walker in his day. Virginia could remember him setting out early in the morning with a packet of sandwiches and not returning until dusk. Virginia herself liked to walk for at least one or two hours. For her, a walk, even through the most familiar streets, was an adventure. She loved seeing people, looking into their faces, and imagining their lives and making up stories about them. Sometimes when she walked she would go into a kind of trance—as she often did when she was writing—and she would begin to talk aloud to herself, startling passersby and getting herself laughed at. Sometimes when she was walking she *was* writing—revising sentences she had written that morning, working out scenes in her head.

Leonard, who also liked a good walk, sometimes accompanied Virginia, and several times a day he took their cocker spaniel, Pinka, for a run in Tavistock Square. Being there so often, Leonard had made the acquaintance of the square keeper, a kind of Bloomsbury village gossip from whom Leonard learned much about his neighbors.

Tea was at four-thirty and dinner was at eight, and again the Woolfs often had guests join them for these meals.

The Woolfs had a large circle of friends and received many invitations to go out. They both liked seeing people, and they also liked going out to a concert or a film now and then, but quiet evenings at home were what they cherished most. After dinner Leonard might roll a few cigarettes, and they would sit smoking, reading, or listening to music on the wireless or on the gramophone. Leonard and Virginia were very fond of music. They loved Beethoven. They loved opera.

The Woolfs had a servant named Mabel Haskins. Mabel came every day and shopped and cooked and tidied for them, and of course they could not have lived as they did without her, for if they had had to do their own shopping and cooking and tidying, how much time would have been left for reading and writing and publishing?

The Woolfs had another house, in the village of Rodmell, Sussex, about two hours' drive from Tavistock Square. This was Monk's House, a seventeenth-century cottage neighboring the village churchyard. The rooms of Monk's House were very small, with low timbered ceilings and stone floors. There was a garden hut on the property where Virginia preferred to work in warmer weather ("my outhouse," she called it). The Woolfs had been coming to Rodmell since 1919, and the years had brought many changes. To Monk's House had come in time plumbing, electricity, and refrigeration. Needless to say these modern conveniences made daily life much more comfortable, and the Woolfs were grateful for them. But the years had brought other changes that were not so welcome. Every year this part of the English countryside was a little more built up, and recently a cement plant had been erected right in the middle of what had been a fine view. Already many trees had been killed by the fumes, and the noise and the smell were often intolerable. Also at times intolerable—at least to Virginia—were Rodmell's clamorous children, church bells, and dogs.

The Woolfs went to Rodmell throughout the year, on weekends and holidays and for short vacations, and they spent most of every summer there. At Monk's House they got up at the same hour and followed much the same routine as in London. Here there was a garden, to which Leonard was devoted, and a lush green lawn for playing bowls. There were plum trees and pear trees and apple trees. There were acres and acres of downs and water meadows for rambling. Such walks excited Virginia in a different way from her city walks. Instead of looking at people and making up stories about them, she could go for miles without seeing anyone, save a shepherd. A hare would start at her feet. She would lie in a cornfield and watch cormorants. She would spy a stoat or a badger or a fox, or a kingfisher taking flight over the River Ouse. (Once, walking over the downs, she and Leonard saw a "great yellow green ape" that belonged to a circus and had escaped from its keeper.)

In the country the Woolfs were helped by another charwoman, Louie Everest, and a gardener, Percy Bartholomew. There were fewer social obligations and fewer guests (in fact there was room for only one guest at Monk's House), and Pinka ran free.

About a week after Leonard and Virginia had visited Merton Hall, Leonard received a letter from Victor. The Rothschilds were about to start their trip; they would be abroad for several weeks, and they did not know what to do with Mitz. Remembering how well Mitz and Leonard had got along, Victor wondered whether Leonard would be willing to take her until they returned.

"But what about Pinka?" Virginia said.

At the sound of her name, Pinka, lying on the floor, tipped her eyes upward without lifting her head, and wagged her short tail.

A spaniel was a hunting dog, after all. What if Pinka thought Mitz was game, like the hares she could not be stopped from chasing (and, alas, sometimes catching) in Rodmell? A fine thing it would be to have to tell Victor when he got back that Mitz had been killed. (In all honesty Leonard thought such news would not be received with tears.)

But Leonard was quite sure, as he told Virginia, that if the two animals were introduced to each other properly, indoors, Pinka would be able to make the distinction between house pet and prey, and she would not be the first dog to have done so. As a young man Leonard had worked for the Civil Service, in Ceylon, where he had often seen dogs living amicably among goats, rabbits, and chickens.

"The important thing is to give them time, let them become acquainted at their own pace and not push them at each other."

And off he went to King's Cross Station, where it had been arranged he was to collect Mitz.

When he returned to Tavistock Square, before entering the flat, Leonard took Mitz out of the box in which he had carried her and tucked her into his waistcoat. Virginia was not home; the Woolfs were making their summer move to Rodmell the next day, and she had a number of errands to do before they left. Leonard went into the sitting room and straight to his usual chair. He sat down, picked up *The Times,* and began to read.

It was the hottest hour of a very hot day, and Pinka lay stretched on the floor, panting and dozing. Mitz stayed where she was, her head peering out from the top of Leonard's waistcoat. She was shivering. Leonard could feel the tiny vibration against his breastbone, and it occurred to him that, hot though it might be, for Mitz, who belonged in the tropics, England would always be chilly.

Half an hour passed. Mitz was unaware of Pinka. Pinka was unaware of Mitz. Then Pinka decided it was time for a walk. She stood up, yawned, shook herself, and padded over to Leonard's chair.

Leonard folded his newspaper and laid it aside. For the first time the animals saw each other.

What? Pinka barked, taking two steps back. She cocked her head from side to side—and the same train of thought that had run through Virginia's mind a week ago in the garden of Merton Hall now ran through Pinka's: Was it a squirrel? Was it a rat?

At such a moment, for a dog, only one thing will do, and that is a good long sniff. Pinka stood up on her hind legs and placed her paws on Leonard's knees. Leonard could feel Mitz cringe against his ribs as the great hairy face drew near. But he kept perfectly still, all nonchalance: didn't every man have a marmoset's head growing out of his bosom?

Mitz kept still too, never taking her eyes off the round black wet snuffling thing that was coming at her. And when the round black wet snuffling thing arrived, she attacked.

Pinka reared back. It was not a hard bite. It was a very small bite made by very small teeth and had not really hurt Pinka. Nevertheless it *was* a bite and must be protested. Pinka threw back her head and howled. And, cool as you please, setting his paper aside, Leonard said, "Go for a walk? Yes, of course. Let's all go together."

Once outside, distracted by the smells of Tavistock Square, Pinka forgot all about Mitz. While Pinka was dashing about the flower beds, Leonard introduced Mitz to the square keeper, and by that evening all Bloomsbury knew about its tiny new resident.

And that evening Virginia discovered what a disconcerting thing it is to dine across from a husband with a monkey's head growing out of his bosom. She was perhaps even more disconcerted by the expression on Mitz's face.

"What a mournful little thing! She looks as if she'd just

lost her best friend. She looks as if she's got the weight of the world on her shoulders."

Only after dinner did Leonard take the chance of putting Mitz down on the sitting-room floor. At first she sat still, curled in a ball, and allowed Pinka to sniff her. But when Pinka opened her jaws and tried to take the ball into her mouth, she got another bite—on the tongue, this time—and this one did hurt.

Pinka's protests shook the house and sent Mitz scurrying under a chair. Leonard called Pinka to him and comforted her with a good scratching round her ears. Meanwhile, he asked Virginia to go down to the basement and fetch a large old wicker birdcage that had been there when they moved in and that they had never got round to throwing out. Virginia brought the cage upstairs and set it on a small table next to Leonard's chair. She got out Mabel's sewing basket and took from it several large scraps of silk. She spread these scraps on the bottom of the cage.

By now Leonard had coaxed Mitz out from under the chair and was trying to feed her, as he had tried unsuccessfully to do several times earlier that day. To his relief, she finally accepted some biscuit and orange rind. When she had eaten her fill, he placed her in the cage, and, after a fastidious inspection of the premises and rearrangement of silk scraps, she curled into a tight ball and went to sleep.

This was how it would be. During the day Mitz and Leonard were inseparable. She stayed either tucked in his waistcoat or perched on his shoulder, her long tail hanging like a braid down his back or wound about his neck. But every evening at sundown she went to her cage, where she stayed until the next morning. The door of the cage was always kept open, and it was easy for Mitz to get to it, jumping from floor to chair to table. In this way she could get away from Pinka whenever she wished. But within days Mitz had grown quite used to Pinka and would never find it necessary to nip her again.

As for Pinka, she knew Mitz's smell now, and she knew Mitz's tiny teeth, and what more was there to know? Pinka understood, just as Leonard had said she would, that Mitz was not a squirrel or a rabbit to be chased. But neither was she someone to run or tumble with, like the dogs Pinka met every day in the square. Indeed, Mitz, hardly bigger than one of Pinka's feathered paws, was too small to play with. This being the case, Pinka quickly lost interest.

"But do you think Pinka likes Mitz?" Virginia asked Leonard.

"Yes, I do."

"And how can you tell?"

"Well, watch: whenever Pinka hasn't seen Mitz for a while and then sees her again, she wags her tail."

And Virginia watched, and it was so.

3

Now that Mitz was in his care, Leonard discovered that she was in worse health than he had thought. She still hobbled when she moved quickly. Her joints were swollen. Her eyes and her fur were lusterless. She had dandruff. She had eczema. (Pinka, too, had once had eczema, and Leonard recognized the scaly pink patches.) And only now did he discover an ugly sore under Mitz's chin, probably caused by the same chain that had rubbed away the fur of her neck. Leonard washed the sore with soap and hot water three times a day. The eczema he treated by dabbing it with cotton soaked in olive oil. Lack of vitamin D was the cause of the rickets, and Leonard knew the cure. He took Mitz out every day, letting her take the sun on his shoulder, and every day he fed her a spoonful of cod-liver oil and some butter.

The Woolfs were now ensconced in Rodmell, but from time to time one or both of them would have to return to

London for some engagement. On the first of these trips, Leonard went to the London Zoo. Like many people, Leonard had mixed feelings about zoos. On the one hand he did not like to see any animal forced to spend its life behind bars. On the other he was fascinated by animals and animal behavior and could not get enough of observing them. Leonard had traveled much in his life, and in many cities he had visited he had been to the zoo. And he believed that you could tell a lot about a city's people from its zoo. In the London Zoo he saw a "microcosm of London" itself: clean, proper, orderly, where "even the lions, as a rule, behave as if they had been born in South Kensington."

That day he went straight to the monkey pavilion and sought out the keeper, a man cast in the same mold as the square keeper: a dry, down-to-earth chap who loved to talk.

"Drafts!" said the zookeeper, wagging a forefinger. "That's what you have to watch out for." Damp, chilly weather (London weather!) could be the death of a monkey. Very small monkeys (and marmosets were among the smallest monkeys in the world) were not very hardy, and all monkeys were sensitive to drafts. Marmosets caught cold easily and were vulnerable to pneumonia and consumption. Their nerves were not strong. They had been known to drop dead out of trees at the sight of a leopard's eyes shining in the dark.

According to the zookeeper, Mitz came from somewhere along the coast of Brazil. Natives caught marmosets in the jungle and sold them for a song to sailors, who in turn hoped to sell them for a great deal more back home. Many of the monkeys got rickets from being kept in the dark for months, first in the holds of ships and later in warehouses. The zookeeper guessed that probably half of them died en route, some of them literally frightened to death. "And half the ones that survive have the pneumonia and don't live very long." He recommended a diet of fruits and vegetables, both raw and cooked, hard-boiled eggs, and liver. He cautioned Leonard to go easy on the milk. Too much could cause diarrhea. "Too much banana ain't good, neither."

But in fact Leonard had discovered a strange thing about Mitz: though she loved all other fruits, she would not eat banana. Given a piece she would either ignore it or, stranger still, take it into her mouth and spit it out forcefully.

The zookeeper said he had never heard of a monkey that did not like banana. "She'll eat insects when she catches 'em," he said. "Oh, you won't be seeing many spiders in your flat no more. And don't be alarmed should you discover her one day chewing on a mouse." The zookeeper said he had seen marmosets pluck sparrows right out of the air and devour them.

"Good luck with her—and mind you don't get too attached, and don't take it too hard if you lose her. Here, we've never been able to keep one alive for more than four years. They don't belong in England, you know. This ain't no climate for 'em. Summer's one thing, but come winter . . ." And he shook his head.

The first thing Leonard did when he got back to Rodmell was to move Mitz's cage away from the window. Then he boiled an egg and fed it to her along with some apple slices for lunch. As always, he was fascinated to watch Mitz eat. The rapid working of her mouth and jaws was almost that of a mechanical thing. Like Virginia, Leonard found Mitz's gluttony somewhat unsettling. Not even the one who fed her was to be trusted. She would snatch the food and move quickly away, glancing back at him over her shoulder, as if she were afraid he would snatch the food back. This brought back to him a heart-breaking memory from Ceylon. He had once given bread to a beggar urchin who had run into an alley and gobbled it down with just such fearful glances over his shoulder.

"What I want to know," said Virginia, "is whether the males really do help the females give birth." It was true—Leonard had remembered to ask the zookeeper. As the mother gave birth—almost always to twins and some-times to triplets—the father would take them from her and wash them. Then, while the young were growing up, it was the father who carried them about, on his shoul-ders or his back, handing them over to the mother only at feeding time.

"Now, that is advanced," said Virginia. "Do other mon-keys do that?" It seemed they did not. And here was another interesting thing about Mitz: unlike other mon-keys, who had fingernails and toenails, like people, Mitz had claws, like Pinka, on all except her great toes. On her great toes, oddly enough, Mitz had nails. Mitz was also unlike other New World monkeys in that she did not have a prehensile tail. Long as it was, it was useless for hanging.

Mitz could climb trees, though, as she nimbly demon-strated in the garden of Monk's House.

The Woolfs had been happy to learn that Mitz was not afraid of cars. Driving to Rodmell she rode all the way on Leonard's shoulder—she seemed to enjoy it particularly when the top of their Lanchester convertible was cranked back. But at Monk's House she had the bad habit of escaping into the garden and climbing trees all the way to the highest branch, and then they had quite a time getting her down again. When calling and tongue-clicking did not work, Leonard resorted to temptation. He put a bit of honey or tapioca pudding (her favorite foods) into the lid of a tin and put the lid in the bottom of a butterfly net. He leaned a ladder against the tree and climbed it, holding the food out to Mitz. Down she came, to be caught in the net.

As many times as Leonard played this trick on Mitz, she never seemed to hold it against him.

But there were times when even temptation did not work. For a half hour or more, Leonard would stand on the ladder, looking up through the leaves at Mitz looking back down at him in wonderment, as if she could not imagine what her man was doing down there waving that silly net.

One Sunday evening, just as the Woolfs were getting ready to drive back to London, Mitz escaped from the house and immediately raced up the lime tree that stood by the gate. While Leonard went to fetch some honey and the butterfly net, Virginia went back into the house to dash off a letter to her sister. She had written four sheets, and still Mitz had not come down from the tree. His patience at an end, Leonard had a stroke of genius.

"Virginia!" he called, clambering down his ladder.

"Yes, Mongoose?" (Mongoose was Virginia's pet name for Leonard.)

"Would you come out here for a moment, please?"

Virginia laid down her pen and went out into the garden.

"Come here," Leonard said. And Virginia went to stand under the tree beside him.

"Closer," he said. Virginia moved closer.

Now, Mitz was a jealous creature, and whenever Leonard showed affection toward his wife in Mitz's presence, Mitz would jump onto his shoulder and protest in her high-pitched staccato way. Seeing Virginia move so close to Leonard now, Mitz climbed down a few branches.

Seeing Leonard put his arm around Virginia, Mitz dropped lower still.

Seeing Leonard nuzzle Virginia's cheek, Mitz shrieked and leapt onto Leonard's shoulder.

Unlike the sweets-in-the-butterfly-net trick, this one worked every time.

4

One afternoon Virginia and Pinka walked to Charleston, arriving in time for tea. Charleston, Vanessa's country retreat, which she shared with her companion, Duncan Grant, was about four miles from Monk's House. In London Vanessa and Duncan lived in Fitzroy Street, not far from Tavistock Square. Virginia and Vanessa were as close as two sisters can be. Vanessa was the elder by three years. Everyone called her Nessa, but to Virginia she was also Dolphin, and to Vanessa Virginia was usually Goat (these were names from their childhood).

Charleston was like no other house in England— Vanessa and Duncan had seen to that, decorating every inch of it—walls to windowsills—with their own hands. Virginia never ceased to be ravished by such a profusion of pattern and color, and always after coming home from Charleston her own house looked to her very plain and dull. But that was also how she looked to herself: very plain and dull beside Vanessa—a goddess in Virginia's eyes, a radiant madonna, a complete woman, impossible not to envy. Vanessa had what people insisted could not be had: her art *and* her children.

At tea they discussed the same things they usually discussed: Vanessa's painting, Virginia's writing, family, friends.

"And how is the marmoset?" Vanessa asked.

"Very well, thank you," Virginia said. "She was in rather bad shape when we got her, but Leonard has done such a wonderful job, she's quite fine now."

"Well, I'm not surprised," Vanessa said, slyly. "He's had such a lot of experience with—monkeys!"

At this Virginia began to laugh. Cup and saucer clattered like false teeth, making her laugh even harder. "With nervous—s-sickly—s-s-sensitive monkeys—don't you mean!" Virginia spluttered, tea sloshing at every word.

And the sisters laughed and laughed.

As a child Virginia had been known to her family as Apes. To her sister she was not only Goat but also Singe, which is French for monkey, and to her husband she was Mandril. (A mandrill is a large, ferocious baboon.) To her intimate friend Vita Sackville-West she was Potto, and a potto is a kind of lemur—not a spaniel, as one of Virginia's biographers thinks—and a lemur, though not a true monkey, is a very close relation.

Yes, Leonard was an excellent nurse, as who should know better than Virginia? Hadn't he seen her through countless bouts of migraine and flu (to both of which she was unusually susceptible), as well as through more serious troubles? All her life Virginia had been plagued by illness. Different doctors had given different opinions. One said it was her heart, another said it was her lungs, a third thought the problem must be psychological. Fevers, tremors, insomnia, swoons, galloping pulse, splitting head, loss of appetite—on the symptoms, at least, all could agree. One endless summer she had lain in bed, as sick as she would ever be, and heard the birds singing in Greek and King Edward VII babbling obscenities. (Years later, when Vita was writing a book about Joan of Arc, Virginia would say, "I could tell you all about her Voices by the way.") A fragile mind in a fragile body, Virginia was. It was because of this that the Woolfs had decided not to have children. As there was no definitive diagnosis, there was no cure. At various times she was treated with laudanum and Veronal, influenza germs, milk, and digitalis. But experience had shown that the best thing for Virginia's health was Leonard's patient loving care.

Now, under the same care, Mitz was thriving. The sore on her neck was almost healed. The eczema was fading. Her eyes gleamed like glass buttons; her fur had a sheen. The swelling round her joints was gone. Gone, too, was the look of perpetual dolor. Now Mitz looked as monkeys should look: lively, sharp, curious. Gone was her hobble. She moved with ease. She had energy. She had spunk.

"Victor will be pleased," Virginia said. They had had a letter from Victor only yesterday: the Rothschilds would be returning to England in about a week.

Leonard had predicted that Pinka would do Mitz no harm. He might have gone further and predicted that the two animals would become friends. But he would not have gone so far as to predict what in fact happened: Mitz grew passionately fond of Pinka.

Pinka (also called Pinker) was eight years old—past

the prime of a dog's life, and, as with many a human past his or her prime, she was overweight and her sight was failing. She had been a gift from Vita, whose own spaniel, Pippin, had had a litter. The Woolfs were enchanted. "An angel of light," Virginia called her. "Leonard says seriously she makes him believe in God . . . and this after she has wetted his floor 8 times in one day." (Virginia was prone to exaggeration.)

Over the years Leonard had nursed Pinka through eczema, worms, lice, heat, motherhood, rheumatism, and a bad paw.

And how could anyone ever repay such a gift? If you are Virginia Woolf, it might be with a book: *Orlando*, a novel inspired by Vita and about Vita and dedicated to her ("the longest and most charming love letter in literature," Vita's son Nigel Nicolson has called it).

As Vita was the model for Orlando, so Pinka was the model for Flush. *Flush*, the biography of Elizabeth Barrett Browning's cocker spaniel, was Virginia's latest book. In a letter to Frederick B. Adams, an American who had written to inquire about the original manuscript, which he was thinking of buying, Virginia explained that she had come upon the idea of writing a life of Flush while reading the letters of Elizabeth Barrett and Robert Browning. "But in fact very little is known about him, and I have had to invent a good deal." Virginia counted among her inspirations the lives written by her dear old friend Lytton Strachey, now, alas, dead. His *Eminent Victorians*, his *Queen Victoria* (dedicated to Virginia)—these were the models she claimed to have in mind when she sat down to *Flush*.

The book was begun as a relaxation—something to cool a brain that had seethed and bubbled over during the feverish labor of completing *The Waves*. The gods of literature punish writers who begin books in this spirit. Lightly though she took it at first, calling it a lark, a *jeu d'esprit*, it soon turned into what all book writing always turns into: work, work, work. And soon enough she is bemoaning: how endless the writing and the rewriting, how tedious the research, how dull and slow the whole business and how she longs only to be quit of it—until it comes as no surprise to find her referring in her diary to "that abominable dog Flush."

And when she finally had finished the book came a further ordeal: the anxious waiting to see what would happen to it. Virginia never allowed anyone to read a book of hers before it was done. Now strangers would paw it. Critics would claw at it. There would be reviews. As always, Virginia braced herself. Leonard, as always, held her hand. Virginia herself had already disparaged the book as "a joke," "a waste," "a bore"—"silly," "foolish," "witless," and "too long"—but, oh, did that mean she was pleased to have Rebecca West agree, in a review in the *Daily Telegraph*, suggesting that it was a joke that should never have left the room where it was born? West was not alone in her criticism. (Another reviewer wept crocodile tears: as a serious writer Mrs. Woolf was now dead.) But in the literary world Virginia had many friends and admirers, and these friends and admirers praised the book to the skies. (Why was it, she wondered, that criticism was always "either mere slobber or mere abuse"?) Joke though *Flush* might be, it was a joke that sold, and sold, as she had known it would. The Book Society chose it for their Book of the Month. Ha-ha! The American Book-of-the-Month Club wanted it, too.

Virginia Woolf was a liar, declared Dame Rebecca West

on television five decades later: She said I have hairy arms, and I don't have hairy arms.

Mr. Adams decided not to buy the manuscript of *Flush* after all.

Mitz would sit for hours going through Pinka's soft wavy coat, separating the hairs with her claws, searching for fleas. When she found one, she would pop it into her mouth. It was a service for which Pinka was no doubt grateful, and the Woolfs should have been grateful, too. And yet it was a disconcerting sight in one's sitting room and took some getting used to. This business is called grooming, and it is a sign of love. (And if there was any mystery as to whom Mitz loved best: she spent most of her time grooming herself.)

Every morning when Leonard came downstairs, Mitz would hop onto his shoulder and groom the sleep out of his eyes. Evenings, as he sat reading, she would sit on his shoulder or on the back of his chair and go through his hair, just as she went through Pinka's. Virginia did her best to ignore them but could not help being alarmed when Mitz would find something and examine it for a long, suspenseful moment before popping it into her mouth. Leonard no longer has to worry about dandruff, she announced to astonished friends.

Another thing that took some getting used to was Mitz's noise. Virginia was a skittish person—hardly less skittish than Mitz herself—easily startled by any loud noise or sudden movement, and Mitz's screeching (often the result of *her* having been startled) had made Virginia fling her pen into the air more than once. But Virginia liked Mitz—the Zet, or the Zed, as Virginia sometimes referred to her. The Zet had wet her arm or left a smut on her blotting paper. Virginia bore such annoyances well. Once, when Leonard's niece Philippa was visiting Monk's House and Leonard was not at home, Mitz jumped onto Virginia's head and became hopelessly entangled in her hair. She could not free herself, and the more Virginia and Philippa tugged, the deeper she sank in her claws. Finally they gave up, and Virginia and Philippa sat talking and waiting for Leonard to come to the rescue, which he did in about half an hour.

Virginia was not above teasing her rival, snuggling up to Leonard now and then precisely in order to provoke an outburst. When Mitz was really piqued, her white tufts would erect themselves like a headdress; she would rock back and forth, smacking her lips and sticking her tongue out at Virginia in the lewdest fashion. And Virginia invented a game to play with her—a form of peekaboo. While Leonard sat reading with Mitz on his shoulder, Virginia would stand in front of his chair and dance from side to side, agitating Mitz, who would jump back and forth from one shoulder to the other—until at last Leonard lost patience and cried, *Oh, ladies, please!*

Now, fleas were not the only wonder of Pinka's coat. Remember: Mitz could not bear the cold. It did not take her long to find the warmest place in the house. On cooler, damper evenings—and there are many cool damp evenings in an English summer—the Woolfs would light a fire. Virginia would sit in her chair, reading or perhaps writing in her diary, and Leonard would sit in his chair, reading or writing, too. And on the rug in front of the fire lay Pinka sleeping, and Mitz lay nestled against her. Sometimes the two animals would curl up together in a chair or in Pinka's basket.

And so were they all four in their places this particular evening at Monk's House (more like Monkeys' House now, teased Vanessa) when the telephone rang and Leonard picked up. "Victor! Well, how are you? How was the trip?" After this Leonard was silent for a long time, listening to Victor's reply, which was understandably lengthy, for it had been a long trip. Virginia was writing in her diary. (Virginia believed that a day on which she did not write in her diary was a day wasted; a thing was not real, Virginia believed, unless she had written it down.)

"Hope you'll understand . . . happier here . . . grown awfully fond . . . responsibility . . ."

Though Virginia was not listening to the words, Leonard's meaning sank in.

"So," she said, as he hung up the phone. "Is Victor angry?"

"Not at all, not at all." Leonard clasped his hands behind his head and leaned back with a satisfied air. It was just as he had suspected: Victor was relieved.

5

In October the Woolfs returned to London bearing a heavy grief. Their friend Roger Fry had died in September. They had reached the age when the death of friends had to be expected. It seemed only yesterday—and not more than two years ago—that they had lost Lytton.

Virginia had admired Roger, as a critic and as a painter—the most intelligent of her friends, she called him. Twenty years ago Roger and Vanessa had been lovers. They had remained close until he died, and now a good part of Virginia's suffering was seeing how Vanessa suffered. She knew that Roger had hoped that she would one day write his biography, and one day she would; but for now all she could do was mourn.

In the wider world, too, there was ample cause for dismay. In Germany the Nazis had gone from strength to strength and were rapidly building up armaments. There was rattling of sabers in Italy as well. On a state visit to

France, the king of Yugoslavia had been slain, along with the French foreign minister, by a Croatian nationalist. It was beginning to look as if only a miracle would preserve peace.

The Woolfs did what they always did in the face of despair: they threw themselves into their work. Leonard became even busier with the political activities to which he had devoted much of his life, serving on committees, giving speeches, writing journalism—and it was he who did most of the work of the Press. He began writing a book, an attack on Nazism and fascism to be called *Quack, Quack!*

Virginia was also writing a book, a new novel for which she had not yet settled on a title.

By this time, Virginia had published ten books of fiction, including her masterpieces *To the Lighthouse* and *The Waves.* Her reputation was secure. In our own day the eminent critic Harold Bloom would find a place for her in his canon, between D. H. Lawrence and James Joyce (about both of whom Virginia herself had her doubts). Canonization would not have surprised her; she knew her work would endure. (A high point of that autumn was a meeting with Yeats at Lady Ottoline Morrell's—and hadn't the great man himself praised *The Waves?*) But: her picture on the side of a bus driving down Manhattan's Fifth Avenue? What would Virginia have thought of this—she who had declined to sit for her portrait for the National Portrait Gallery? That one or another of her books might be made into a film—this would not have surprised her; it was something that was already happening to books back then. But: She and her friends—Vita and Ottoline and Tom and Lytton and Carrington—impersonated on stage and screen? A 1990s fall fashion collection inspired by a film about Carrington—tweed suits and velvet coats and rooster-feathered hats that Carrington would not have been caught dead in but that might indeed have been worn by Vita or Ottoline or Lady Colefax? What would Virginia Woolf have said to all this?

At the time we are talking about, however, it was not homage that was on Virginia's mind: it was hostility. Here she was, in a new book by Wyndham Lewis, raked over the coals. The length of a chapter needed to say that her work was of no significance at all. Here was Bloomsbury mocked and reviled—not for the first time or the last. But *this* time she would fight back. She would defend herself, she would. She would publish a letter—

No, she would not. Not for the first time or the last, Leonard stopped her. She must not let herself be baited, he said. To let herself be dragged into public controversy would only make things worse. Well, then, what should she do about such abuse? Pay no attention, get on with her work. And if she couldn't work, what then? If such attacks upset her so that she couldn't write—what then, Mongoose, what then? Then she should read until she could write again; that's what books were for.

So they discussed it, husband and wife, writer and writer, as they walked round the Serpentine and Kensington Gardens. (From time to time came a familiar interruption: "Pardon, sir, but could you tell me, please—what is that animal?") This was their way: whenever Virginia had what they called "a thorn," she and Leonard would talk things over and try to get the thorn out. But today she needed more help than usual. She was bristling with thorns today. She was afraid that she had spoiled Leonard's life, with her illnesses and all her need

for care. She had made his life, he said. But without her
he might have done more—traveled more, written more,
achieved more in politics. She had not prevented him
from doing anything important, he said.

"Oh, the poor thing!"

"She's not poor and she's not a thing." People's reac-
tions to Mitz often irked Leonard.

"Is it a rat, sir?"

"Now, what do you think I'd be walking about
Kensington Gardens with a rat on my shoulder for?"

Without Leonard, Virginia believed, she would be "a
ravaged sensitive old hack." He was the best and the wisest of husbands ("& I have him every day"). Once, he had
come to the defense of a prostitute who was being bul-
lied by a policeman. He was a man who healed sick animals and grew dahlias and wrote books taking on the
biggest bullies in the world. Her Mongoose.

(The story about the prostitute had got all over town,
for Maynard Keynes's wife, the ballerina Lydia Lopokova,
happened to be passing by and witnessed the whole
episode. It seems that that night the Woolfs had been to
a costume party to which everyone had gone dressed as a
character out of Lewis Carroll. They were on their way
home when they came upon the policeman bullying the
prostitute. Thrusting himself squarely between them,
Leonard had taken the woman's side—so what if he was
wearing a green baize apron and carrying carpenter's
tools? The March Hare stood by, nervously touching its
paws to its ears.)

Oh, he was not perfect, of course—Virginia was not
saying Leonard was perfect. He could be quite irascible.
Hadn't Mabel come to her in tears just the other day?
Oh, how Mr. Woolf had spoken to her! It was a constant

problem. He was mean to servants. It made Virginia very angry. It's your damned inferiority complex, she didn't mind telling him. He had not been brought up with servants, as she had been. He was not comfortable with them, and he took it out on them. With servants he was churlish and suspicious and tyrannical. The wisest and most just of men—but not with Mabel. With Mabel, a bully. It was strange. It was sad. Other people noticed it, too, and Virginia was ashamed for him. No, Leonard Woolf was no saint. But there were times, and they were not rare, when it seemed to Virginia that she was the luckiest wife in England, and that no two people could have been happier.

Besides, there were things Leonard hated about her, too.

She was a snob, he didn't mind telling her. Well, she believed in the virtues of the aristocracy, if that's what he meant. But when asked to say what those virtues were, she was as helpless as Tom Eliot when asked (as he often was asked, by Virginia, who enjoyed teasing him about his religion) to define God. She blathered something about ancient land and ancient blood and centuries of breeding and tradition. But could she say in what way the aristocracy was or had ever been a force for social justice or good? She could not. The way she rhapsodized over blue blood made *his* blood boil. The way she let herself be chased and caught by Sibyl Colefax and dined grandly at her grand house with Noël Coward (who adored her, gushed Sibyl) and then moaned endlessly about her showing off and made endless fun of her—this was insufferable.

It was the snob in Virginia that had fallen in love with Vita, Leonard believed. The emeralds and the pearls, the castles and the gardens, the ancestral home with its 365 rooms and the army of servants to do her bidding—without all this Vita would never have seduced his wife, Leonard believed. "Legs like beech trees" indeed!

So the Woolfs had their differences; there would always be things they deplored in each other, things they would never understand. But about their marriage Leonard agreed with Virginia: he did not know two people who were happier together.

"Look, Nurse! That man has a bat on his shoulder!"

Arm in arm round Kensington Gardens, with the wind blowing and the leaves scattering and Pinka lunging at the ducks. Yes, this was their way: walking and talking, until all the thorns were out. Then home. No guests for dinner tonight; no party to go to. It would be one of their blessed quiet evenings alone. Roast chicken and apple tart. More talk—plans—dreams. They should start saving up for a big trip—oh, to go someplace far away and very strange—India or China or America. After dinner Leonard would make them cigarettes. She would read her Shakespeare and he his Spengler. The animals would snuggle before the fire—

"Pardon, sir, but why doesn't your dog eat that animal, sir?"

"Why should she?"

6

"*You* don't suppose Mitz minds how far she's come down in the world?" Virginia said. She was thinking of their own humble dwelling compared with Merton Hall. The Woolfs knew many people besides the Rothschilds who lived in luxurious style. Coming home once from Vita's Sissinghurst Castle, Virginia declared herself "positively ashamed of my middle class origin." But in fact the Woolfs preferred their cottage to any castle. And castles being such drafty places, and drafts being what Mitz must above all avoid, it's not likely she would have been happy in one either. Besides, Mitz herself was of humble origins. Among the Callitrichidae, she belonged with the common marmosets. The Callitrichidae have their aristocrat: the golden lion marmoset—a brilliant creature that does indeed resemble a miniature lion, with a lustrous silky coat and a mane like burnished copper threads. It was one of these dandies that was the first marmoset ever to be seen in Europe. This was in the mid-eighteenth century. It ended up, appropriately, in the court of Louis XV, where it spent much of its time nestled in the bosom of the Marquise de Pompadour.

A monkey needs exercise, or it will develop arthritis. Though still most often to be found on Leonard's shoulder, indoors Mitz was free to roam. This was not without danger: she might easily be trampled. In fact she seemed always to be getting underfoot and it was impossible *not* to step on her now and then. Nor was this the only difficulty. For weeks after Mitz's arrival, Mabel received "the fright of me life" three times a day.

Crash!

"I couldn't help it, Mrs. Woolf. I opened the cupboard and she jumped straight out at me—almost like she did it on purpose."

It was Mabel who lived out the zookeeper's prediction and one day discovered Mitz chewing on a mouse. The Woolfs found her clutching her broom for support, ashen and gibbering. *Fright of me life—the whole head bit off—dripping blood—still alive—and the little tail lashing—* The Woolfs were spared the grisly sight: Mitz had fled the commotion to finish the mouse in peace.

"You mean to say that you have never seen a cat that has caught a mouse?"

This was Leonard, very cold and deliberate: a prosecutor interrogating a witness.

"Of course I have, sir."

"And did you carry on then in this absurd manner—did you shriek like a madwoman?"

"It's not the same, sir."

"It is."

"Oh, it isn't."

"It most certainly is. If you'll just think for one second—"

Here Virginia, fearing it would be Mabel's head off next, suggested she get on with her sweeping.

"Stupid woman," Leonard muttered as he stomped back to his room.

"Brute," Virginia muttered at his back.

It was clear that Leonard was not going to tolerate any squeamishness about Mitz.

"I'm sorry," said a bookkeeper whom they had recently hired for the Press. "But I have trouble concentrating with that animal running about loose."

"Oh, what a shame," she was told. "And just when we thought you were going to work out."

In the country, where things were always calmer, Louie was calmer too, accommodating to Mitz more quickly than Mabel did. Discovering Mitz in the kitchen one day chewing on a lizard, she had the good sense to go busy herself in another room for a bit.

You can teach a monkey to do many things, but alas not the one thing most desirable. Leonard knew this and did not even try. Living with Mitz meant constantly cleaning up after her—nothing else to be done. Virginia took this admirably in her stride, but the chars complained about muck on their freshly mopped floors or in even more unseemly places. "Don't blame me," Mabel grumbled, "if it doesn't one day get stirred into the hash."

Percy the gardener was fond of Mitz and got in the habit while working of filling his pockets with worms and slugs to feed to her later. Leonard did the same, and herein is the source of the widespread rumor that Woolf once arrived at a luncheon of the Rodmell Labour Party crawling with bugs (he had forgotten all about them).

Among the Woolfs' friends and relations, Mitz was more tolerated than loved. "Ugly," "horrid," "hideous," she was called. Much fun was made of the patches of old mackintosh Leonard tried sewing onto the sleeves of some of his jackets, for waterproofing. A joke went about that soon they would see Mitz sculpted in the hedges of Monk's House (topiary was one of Leonard's hobbies). Before the Woolfs were married, Vanessa had told Leonard that he was the only man she could imagine as her sister's husband (this despite Lytton Strachey's description of him as a man who would murder his wife). But with time she championed him less and less. Dolphin and Mongoose got on each other's nerves, as in-laws will. Mitz did not help matters. Vanessa was counting on an early demise—the marmoset of Kensington days had survived only briefly—but: "that horrid little monkey . . . still thrives however much Leonard treads on him."

Vanessa's son Quentin so detested Mitz that, sixty years later, he would remember her with similar nastiness: "One always hoped for a severe frost that would finish Mitz, but Leonard took infinite pains to keep it well wrapped up in a cosy place."

Ethel Smyth came to visit Virginia soon after Mitz had arrived. Virginia had told her about Mitz, but Ethel either had forgotten (she was old) or perhaps had not heard (she was deaf). Ethel was sitting on the sofa, talking. She had her ear trumpet in, though she did not need it, as she was talking on and on, about herself as usual, and all the listening was as usual up to her hostess. It was the ear trumpet that attracted Mitz, who had seen plenty of humans but never one with a horn. As Ethel was venting herself—a conductor had slighted her, a critic had failed to recognize her genius—Mitz stole onto the sofa beside her. Twice Virginia tried to alert Ethel, but Ethel would not be interrupted. Then, going to brush what she thought was a fly from her arm (Mitz had rested a paw there), Ethel screamed. Mitz screamed back (*right* into the trumpet) and dashed under the sofa. Ethel shot her feet in the air. Toppling onto her side, she struggled to regain balance and dignity, furiously kicking her short legs.

Virginia laughed. She tried not to, of course, but it was useless. Each time she started to apologize, she choked. When she had finally got herself under control, it was too late.

And so Mitz accomplished that day what Virginia never could: she got "the old turkey cock" to stop talking and leave.

After this, Ethel would not set foot in the house until Mitz had been locked in the WC.

Tom Eliot, that most fastidious man, and a frequent guest of the Woolfs in those days, was surprisingly accepting of Mitz. He was always polite to her and did not even mind when she untied his shoelaces under the dining table. Once, when he was staying the weekend at Monk's House, he went to pet her and she bit him, but instead of becoming angry he exclaimed: "'How shall I hold the little marmouset, if you devour first one of my hands, then the other?'" (Richardson. The "marmouset" addressed here is not a monkey, however, but a woman.)

After Tom brought his friend Emily Hale to see the Woolfs, she described Mitz sitting on Leonard's shoulder "peering out at one, first from one side, then the other," and how she found Mitz's "long tail[,] which hangs down from his master's neck like a short queue, slightly confusing at first."

It should not have irked Virginia that of all their friends Mitz seemed to like Sibyl Colefax best, but it did. When Mitz jumped into Sibyl's expensive tweed lap, Virginia wickedly wished for the unmentionable. Sibyl, though she did not return Mitz's affection, was indulgent, rattling her pearls and letting Mitz paw them (Mitz loved pearls—and how was she to know, as Virginia did, thanks to Vita, that these were fakes?). Mitz liked Vita too, scampering up and down those famous legs—truly like beech trees now that Vita (as Virginia noted with a pang) had grown stout.

The presence of Ottoline Morrell always excited Mitz. (Was Mitz a snob? She seems to have been quite partial to ladyships.) It may have been the Pinka-colored hair, the ostrich feathers, or the pearls galore; it may have been the cooing-wooing voice—or perhaps Mitz sensed the generous heart that lay beneath those gaudy brocades. Like no one else Ottoline fussed over Mitz, sighing, "Oh, you dear little thing, you dear sweet darling little thing," while Leonard restrained himself, gripping his hands together behind his back. (Some slyboots suggested that Mitz's shaggy white tufts may have reminded Ott of her old flame Bertie Russell.)

"I could never look long upon a monkey," wrote Congreve, "without very mortifying reflections." Virginia looked long upon Mitz very often. She wondered about Mitz as she had wondered about the cats and dogs she had known all her life. What was it like to be an animal? How did the world look through a dog's eyes? What did cats think of us? Without such wonder, it is doubtful Virginia ever would have written *Flush*. Now it was Mitz's walnut of a head she wished to crack. Did marmosets dream? Did they remember? Did they regret? What did marmosets want?

Virginia was glad when Mitz was used to her enough to let her bring her face right up to Mitz's and look into her eyes. She liked to stare into Pinka's eyes too, but you cannot lock gazes with a dog the way you can lock gazes with a cat or, as she now discovered, with a marmoset. (In another day, another name for marmoset was Egyptian cat.) When Virginia stared hard and unblinking into Mitz's eyes, Mitz stared hard and unblinking back. Sometimes, after a minute or so, Mitz would dart forward and bite the tip of Virginia's nose—just as a cat will sometimes do. ("Cats and monkeys, monkeys and cats—all human life is there." Was Henry James *ever* wrong?)

Pinka's eyes were the very image of trust—never so much as when she tipped them up at you. But Virginia had never seen such an expression in Mitz's eyes; always a glint of suspicion, a cast of doubt. Virginia observed also that, unlike Pinka, Mitz was never wholly relaxed; even asleep she remained tense, curled in that tight little ball. When Virginia joked about how much she and Mitz had in common, she was right. Two nervous, delicate, wary females, one as relentlessly curious as the other. Both in love with Leonard—for both, he was their rock, their "inviolable centre." They both were mischievous. They both had claws.

Watching her with Pinka, Virginia wondered how Mitz would behave with her own kind. She would have given much to be able to observe Mitz in her natural habitat.

"Mongoose, what would happen if Mitz were returned to the wild?"

"She would be terrified. She would never survive."

So: she could never go home again. But did she want to? Was that why she was forever trying to run out the door—was she trying to find her way home?

South America. Virginia had been there, in her imagination; she had set part of her first novel in South America, though she knew almost nothing about the place. She had once been moved to describe Vanessa as "a South American forest, with panthers sleeping beneath the trees." One of the loveliest gifts she would ever receive was a framed glass box of South American butterflies, from her Argentine admirer Victoria OCampo. ("Recognize anyone?" said Virginia, lifting Mitz up to where the case hung on the wall.)

Time passed, and even Mabel grew accustomed to Mitz at last. "It's like we always had her, isn't it?" she said one day. And so it was.

Though he continued to care for her, seeing scrupulously to all her small needs, and though he too enjoyed watching her, Leonard never indulged in speculations about Mitz's inner life. It was not his way. But for Virginia this habit of musing and "making up" came as naturally as breathing.

Sitting in her sunlit room, she sees a prehistoric shadow moving on the wall—a mighty beast, a dinosaur-ape is lumbering toward her. Then, light as a moth, Mitz lands on her desk—Shakespeare's "nimble marmazet." Virginia thrusts her nose right up to the flat naked gray mask. "How do I look to thee, Mitzi: ugly, horrid, hideous? And why dost thou hate banana?"

But only think, said Virginia: Mitz had already seen more of the world and survived more adventures than most people do in a lifetime. Born into one of Earth's great paradises, she had been captured and taken by ship all the way across the Atlantic and up the Thames to the Port of London. Imprisoned in a junk shop, she had been rescued, as in a fairy tale, from almost sure death by the richest young man in England. Living in the lap of luxury yet languishing still, she had been rescued once again and brought to Bloomsbury, the very heart (Virginia did not blush to call it) of literary, artistic, and intellectual Britain.

So why don't you write her biography? said Vanessa, not without tartness. But of course what Virginia really wanted was for Mitz to write her own.

The Pargiters had been Virginia's first title for her novel-in-progress, but by this time she was calling it *Here & Now*. She would say that no book of hers had given her more pleasure and excitement to write—and she would say that no book of hers had given her more anguish. She had plans for other books, too: Roger Fry's biography, a sequel to *A Room of One's Own*, and a collection of essays on fiction (the only one of these books that she would not finish). Other writers worried about running out of ideas, but Virginia knew that she would never live long enough to write all the books that she had in her.

Usually, she worked on fiction in the morning and on nonfiction after lunch. (Leonard claimed that he could tell whether she had been writing fiction or nonfiction by how flushed she was when she came out of her studio.) She too was a critic, she too reviewed books—and how, by the way, did she judge herself in this role—she who was so sensitive to criticism? Not tough enough, it seems. Too polite. (Ah.)

In *Flush* Virginia describes a house pet mystified by the

activity of a hand perpetually moving a black stick over a white page. Mitz and Pinka were likewise mystified by this activity to which both Leonard and Virginia devoted so much of their time. The two sounds most often heard in that household were: the scratching of pen upon paper, the rustle of pages being turned. To Pinka and Mitz these were reassuring sounds, signifying that all was well, like the faintly clayey smells of books and ink, also comforting and familiar.

Both Tavistock Square and Monk's House were overflowing with books. Guests came and went, bearing books with them, bearing books away. Understood: for Leonard and Virginia and their friends, books were a kind of food. But was it not strange, to have no games— no Fetch the Ball, no Scare the Char? Never to run! Never to climb! Never to dig! And there were other mysteries. Why did it require the ring of a bell to let the Woolfs know someone was at the door? Why did they wonder *who* was at the door when it was obviously Ottoline, reeking of perfume and pug? Here they were asking Mabel what was for lunch—as if they had never smelled sausage and eggs before!

First the leaves were gone from the trees, then they were gone from the ground. It was winter, wet and gray; it was Christmas, and they were back at Rodmell; it was 1935.

The year began with a performance. Virginia had written a play, *Freshwater,* a comedy about her great-aunt Julia Margaret Cameron. On the evening of the eighteenth of January, about eighty people gathered in Vanessa's Fitzroy Street studio to watch the play. Virginia had not neglected to write a part for Mitz. And when Leonard (as Mr. Cameron) spoke his line "[*looking at the marmoset*]

'Life is a dream,'" and Virginia's brother Adrian (as Tennyson) replied "Rather a wet one, Charles," Mitz brought down the house by soaking Leonard's sleeve right on cue.

Leonard finished *Quack, Quack!* at the end of February. Virginia was still struggling with *Here & Now*. Leonard watched this struggle with anxiety. He was alarmed to see Virginia, coming in to lunch after her morning's work, beet red and almost reeling, one hand to her throbbing head and the other to her wildly jigging heart. Some mornings he would not let her work at all; he served her breakfast in bed and insisted that she stay there. No one knew better than he how serious she was about her writing, but she must not be allowed to make herself sick over it. It was making him sick just watching her.

What they both needed was a holiday. And when the daffodils and the hyacinths were in bloom, they began to make plans.

Vanessa had gone to live for six months in Rome. The Woolfs would go visit her. They would drive through Holland, Germany, Austria, cross the Brenner Pass into Italy—

But wait. Germany? Was that wise? From all sides the Woolfs kept hearing that it was not. But the Woolfs would not be daunted. The Woolfs would travel where they pleased, and besides, Leonard wished to see for himself what the political situation in Germany was. Virginia made jokes about ways to hide his nose. Leonard sought the advice of an acquaintance in the Foreign Office, who warned him to avoid any sort of political rally or parade. A meeting was arranged with Prince Bismarck, the counselor at the German Embassy.

Prince Bismarck was all soothing graciousness. A bad idea to visit Germany? Germany unsafe for an English Jew and his wife? Simply false. However, in the event of the kind of trouble that he assured Leonard could not possibly arise, the prince gave him an official letter informing All Whom It May Concern that Mr. and Mrs. Woolf were to be treated with every respect, etc., and provided with every kind of assistance, etc., should they happen, etc., etc.

They set out on the first of May, Leonard, Virginia, and Mitz. Pinka, alas, had to stay behind in Rodmell, with Percy. As they piled their luggage into the back seat, the Woolfs were filled with the high spirits they always experienced at the start of a journey. They did not care at all that they would be missing the Jubilee (it was the twenty-fifth anniversary of the accession to the throne of George V) for which all London was now decked and festooned.

Mitz sat in her usual place, on Leonard's shoulder. But once they were on their way, she would often perch between his hands, on the steering wheel.

"It's all right, girl, they'll be back," Percy said when, having searched every room for the hundredth time, Pinka beseeched him with eloquent eyes: Where is everybody?

7

Holland—that most picturesque of countries, with its tulip fields and windmills and canals and beautiful old houses—charmed the Woolfs. The days were mostly warm, the skies were blue, and they drove almost everywhere with the car open. The cleanliness and comfort of Dutch establishments, the great variety of fine shops, the throngs of cyclists, the Rembrandts and the Vermeers, Dutch conformity and Dutch courtesy—these were some of the things the Woolfs would remember.

In Holland Mitz attracted even greater attention than she did back home. "We are received everywhere like film stars," Virginia wrote to her sister; "a crowd of 20 round the car when we stop. All the children come running; old ladies are sent for ... such is their love of Apes."

After eight days they crossed the border, at Roermond, into—

Another world.

A portrait of Hitler in the customs office; a customs official vituperating a peasant for not removing his cap in front of that portrait.

They were on the road to Cologne when they saw the first sign: JEWS GET OUT OF GERMANY.

"Where is everybody?" Virginia wondered aloud.

Leonard had been wondering the same thing. They had passed Cologne now and were driving toward Bonn. The road was suspiciously empty. And as they neared Bonn, they saw something even more suspicious: armed soldiers lining both sides of the road. What could it mean?

Leonard felt in his pocket for the letter from Prince Bismarck. He did this furtively; he did not want Virginia to know how anxious he was. *Mitz* knew: she could tell from the tightness in Leonard's neck. What was up? Ah, here was a policeman who might explain. But the policeman had no time to explain, only to give orders, and these he shouted: Stop! Go back! The road was closed! *"Der Herr Präsident kommt!"*

The policeman's agitation unnerved Leonard, who turned the car round immediately and looked for a place to park.

Well, here they were in Bonn; might as well get out and have a look.

The first thing they saw was a banner stretched between two lampposts: JEWS GET OUT OF BONN.

They went to see the house where Beethoven was born. Beloved Beethoven—who was German too, they reminded themselves. Afterward, they went to a café. They were tired and thirsty and downcast. Leonard suffered from chronic tremors in both hands and now he was shaking so violently he could barely drink his tea. So:

Herr Präsident was coming. "Well, who could that be but *you-know-who?*" Virginia said, dropping her voice to a whisper (the café was crowded).

Leonard, who had given up trying to conceal his anxiety, said he thought the sooner they got out of Bonn, the better. "We have to find a different road from the one we came in on," he said, taking out his map. They were now on the right bank of the Rhine; they needed to get to the left bank. There they would pick up the road to Mainz.

They left the café and with the help of a man in the street found their way across a bridge. But when they arrived on the opposite bank they were confronted by a great mob. There were men in uniform—policemen, and soldiers with rifles, like the ones they had seen on the Autobahn before—and rank upon rank of uniformed children. A band was playing, and some people were singing along at the tops of their voices; others were chanting. A rippling red sea of flags. Swastikas, swastikas everywhere, and banners waving—THE JEW IS OUR ENEMY, read one just a few yards away.

Leonard and Virginia sat stunned in their car. They had the top down; they could not have felt more exposed.

"Oh," Virginia said, her voice sounding very far away. "Now what are we going to do?"

"Meet *Herr Präsident,* from the look of it," Leonard muttered. He was sure that this was what the people must be waiting for. Whatever you do, stay away from Nazi demonstrations, he had been warned. And now here they were, stuck in the middle of one. Theirs was the only car on the road. Now people were looking their way. Mitz felt the quickening pulse in Leonard's neck and his repeated swallowing.

Came a man in black uniform, face very red. He threw up his hands, he shook his fists, he lifted one knee and then the other and stamped his feet. He was a swastika himself, all angles, twisted, black and red. He bore down on the car. Leonard felt for the letter in his pocket. Mitz, excited by the noise and the flags and now *this* amusing fellow, leapt onto the steering wheel and screeched. The man stopped in his tracks. Surprise, then puzzlement, then tenderness showed in his face. *"Ah—oh—ah!"* he cried. He clapped his hands like a child. *"Das liebe kleine Ding!"*

It was as if the Woolfs had vanished. The stormtrooper had eyes only for Mitz. He leaned into the car, and Leonard inhaled a mixture of beer, onion, leather, pomade, and sweat. The man wagged a finger at Mitz, and Virginia closed her eyes and sent up a prayer that Mitz would not bite it. Bite it she did, though—but this seemed only to increase his delight. He burbled and cooed, offering wurst fingers to Mitz, one by one. And what was the sweet little creature's name? When he heard it he laughed and repeated it several times, slapping his thigh. He loved it—*loved it!* At last he stepped back from the car, clicked his heels together, and raised his arm. *"Heil Hitler!"*

The Woolfs understood that they were being allowed to drive on. Leonard inched the car forward as the man shouted to the crowd to make way, make way for Mitzi! Many people had caught sight of Mitz now and were pointing at her and crying out. Behind them other people craned their necks for a better view, and the *ohs* and *ahs* grew louder and shriller, and Mitz's name could be heard being passed on. Laughter and cheering and arms shooting out: *"Heil Hitler!" "Heil Hitler!"* Anyone would have thought it was for Mitz the Nazis had gathered today. She had jumped onto Leonard's shoulder again, and she kept moving from one side of his neck to the other and surveying the crowds on either side of the road—she might have been reviewing her troops. Every minute or so she let out one of her high-pitched trilling screams. Virginia was on the verge of screaming, too. It took all her effort to remain composed. She smiled back meekly at the smiling crowd, she lifted her arm: *Heil Hitler!* Numbness in her legs, hands, and face. Sweat tickling her ribs.

They drove on—very slowly, as they had to. They crept along for miles—and still the bands played and the flags waved and The Jews Were Our Enemy and men, women, and children hailed Mitz with the Nazi salute.

When, finally, there came a chance to turn off the road, Leonard took it and stepped on the gas. After they had gone about a mile he stopped the car, and they sat for a few moments staring at each other. They were in that strange place between laughter and tears. "Well," said Leonard, reaching into his pocket for some dried worms to feed Mitz. "Who needs Prince Bismarck?"

"Did we tell you how the marmoset saved us from Hitler?" Virginia would recall (with her usual tendency toward exaggeration) in a letter to a friend written several months later.

In fact it was Göring that the crowd in Bonn had been waiting for.

Of their three days in Germany the Woolfs would remember this: the huge anti-Jewish signs they saw everywhere; how, because of the spectacular distraction created by Mitz, they never had any trouble and no one ever suspected that Leonard was Jewish. (Of course, the Woolfs could have no idea that, a few years later, their names would be placed on a list that the Gestapo had begun to compile: to be arrested immediately upon the invasion of England.)

By the time the Woolfs left Germany, the four words *das liebe kleine Ding* had become so loathsome to Leonard that he feared he might strike the next mouth that uttered them. He had always disliked the silliness Mitz seemed to bring out in people, the stupid questions and comments the sight of her invariably provoked. Abroad, it was only worse: first in Holland, then in Germany, and when they moved on to Austria and Italy it would be much the same. It was not until they were driving back home, along the French Riviera, that they would notice a change. When a hotelkeeper in Draguignan refused to let Mitz into the hotel, it was almost a relief. ("We had at last, after travelling 2,469 miles . . . reached a country in which a marmoset was not a dear, little thing.") The sang-froid with which the French reacted to Mitz increased Leonard's respect for that people immensely.

The Woolfs had reached Innsbruck by the twelfth. The next day they crossed the Brenner Pass and drove to Verona, where they stayed the night. They made their way down to Rome, taking their time (it's the journey not the arrival that matters, as Leonard liked to say, quoting Montaigne). On the sixteenth they arrived in Rome, where Vanessa had booked rooms for them at L'Albergo d'Inghilterra.

Two of Vanessa's children, Quentin and Angelica, were staying with her, and so that first day was a family reunion. When the Woolfs told the story of their adventure in Bonn, Quentin said he did not see how the Germans could have failed to notice Mitz's resemblance to their own Dr. Goebbels.

Fascism was ascendant in Italy at this time, but there was nothing like the atmosphere of tension and menace that had been so thick in the land of the Nazis. The days were lazy, sun filled; the Italians as affable as ever. The Woolfs took in the sights at their ease: the Forum, the Vatican, the Borghese. Virginia practiced her Italian. Hours in a piazza, writing postcards, sipping such coffee as could not be had anywhere back home. The Caffè Greco, Vanessa and Angelica sketching, Virginia reading Stendhal on Rome, the men reading the papers: Lawrence of Arabia had crashed his motorbike. They went to a rag market, and while Vanessa shopped for crockery with her expert, potter's eye, Virginia was struck by a vision of her as she had once been: a young married woman, sumptuous, queenly, serenely in command and trailed by admirers, the most ardent of whom was Virginia herself.

The Woolfs and the Bells said good-bye on the twenty-fourth. Two days later, at Ventimiglia, Leonard and Virginia crossed the border into France. By now they had begun to weary. If the truth be told, more than they wanted to see France they wanted to be home. Their own rooms, their own chairs . . . After all these weeks motoring, the car was like a cage. And they both were itching to be back at work. Even Mitz had had enough and was spending more and more time sleeping in the back seat among the luggage.

The last two days were unbearable. It rained and rained, and the cold was the cold of autumn. There were bright spots, of course. In Chartres they were ravished by two masterpieces: the cathedral, which they had all to themselves that dark rainy day, and a superb meal, with a *sauce crème à la moutarde* that even Virginia would find memorable.

Home. The last day of May. A white mist over Sussex. The Downs so much fuller and greener than when they had left. Approaching Rodmell, they thought about Pinka—how good it would be to see her again. And what about Mitz? Did Leonard think Mitz had missed Pinka? Virginia wanted to know. Had Pinka missed Mitz? Maybe, said Leonard with a yawn; maybe so.

Home!

What was that shovel doing, leaning against the door? Ah, here was Percy. But what—?

Eyes red, mouth grim, Percy stood before them with Pinka's basket in his arms, and in her basket lay Pinka, dead.

8

"Thats very nice of you, about giving L. a dog," Virginia wrote to Vita. "But at the moment I think he feels too melancholy."

She went on to tell Vita the story: How Pinka had been perfectly well until about two weeks after the Woolfs left her with Percy. Then she had a fit, followed by two more. The vet was sent for and was confounded—could it be meningitis? She grew sicker and weaker and refused to eat. She died the night before the Woolfs returned. Now she lay buried in the orchard.

They were both melancholy. It was the last thing they would have thought when they left: never to see Pinka again. They were heartbroken—oh, but they did not want to wallow in their feelings. As much as they liked animals the Woolfs disliked people who were sentimental about them or who cherished them to the point of fetishism. Though neither of them would ever have wanted to live without a dog, they frowned when

Ottoline planted kiss after kiss on the snub nose of her Socrates. They did not like pugs or toy breeds in general. They knew that there was a way to care for animals without treating them like humans, and they were wary of champions of animal rights. The Woolfs knew perfectly well that dogs do not make better friends than people and would have been appalled at the suggestion that Pinka or any other pet could replace the child they had not been able to have. For many people the death of a dog might have been occasion for weeping and wailing, but the Woolfs would not allow themselves that indulgence. They wanted to be better than that.

They had arrived back at Monk's House in the early morning. After they heard Percy's story, they sat down to a wordless, tasteless breakfast, and by eleven Leonard was at his desk. *Quack, Quack!* had been published just the day before, and the *Times Literary Supplement* had printed a tepid review, which Leonard read over breakfast. Then straight off to work on his new book.

As for Virginia, she was feeling much too unsettled to return immediately to her novel. She brooded over the bad side of taking a holiday, how it broke one of the habit of writing—and in writing of course habit was all. And hard as it was to write, not to write was harder by far, and there was always the deep, deep writer's fear that to lose the habit would be to lose the knack. And poor Pinka— oh, here were her pawprints on Virginia's blotting paper!

Back in London a few days later, the Woolfs received more bad news. Mabel had broken the gramophone. Of course it had to be their favorite possession. Leonard was beside himself. This time, he raged, that stupid woman must go—good riddance to her and her impotable coffee!

Well, she did not go, after all; Virginia saved her; but the row was fierce. Virginia did not think she had ever seen Leonard so ugly. She knew that grief over Pinka was partly to blame. There was no doubt he felt the loss more keenly than she did. Yes, they absolutely must get another dog, she told Vita. But not yet.

Now the days wore on: there was the usual shuttling between city and country, the usual visits with the usual people, among whom the most amusing was Tom ("one of 'us,'" Virginia pronounced him), who was having such a success with his *Murder in the Cathedral*. (But when they saw the play that November: "I had almost to carry Leonard out, shrieking," according to Virginia, who liked it hardly better.) Once Virginia did get back to work, it was with a vengeance. She saw her novel finished by the end of summer, but still she had not found a title to please her.

Summer: though a dogless walk was not the same, Regent's Park in June gave exquisite pleasure—oh, how much better to walk than to ride in a car! Sitting in the garden at Monk's House and hearing the larks sing and the bees drone . . . Picking mushrooms and wild straw-berries . . . Seeing the hares race over the gorse . . . And June brought the Glyndebourne Festival, which had opened the summer before and was only five miles from Rodmell. They dressed: she in pale blue silk, he in black broadcloth. They spread a blanket on the lawn by the lake and ate cold ham between acts of *The Magic Flute*. And while Mozart played, all woes were forgotten. Home they went, singing, off-key but happy: "*Mann und Weib, und Weib und Mann . . .*"

And what about Mitz? Did Mitz miss Pinka? The Woolfs wondered about this. It was true that, for some time after they returned from abroad, Mitz did not seem quite herself: she was rather listless and kept more to her birdcage than usual. But Leonard thought this might be only travel fatigue or something like the malaise Virginia often experienced after a holiday. Sometimes, it was true, Mitz would wander about the room, investigating every corner, peering under furniture, as if searching for something she had lost; or she would cross back and forth between Leonard's chair and Virginia's chair, looking from one to the other as if to ask something—but then she had always behaved, as Virginia once wrote, "as if the world were a question."

One evening Mitz sat for a very long time very still on the spot where Pinka's basket had been but was no more (Pinka had been buried in it). Melancholy indeed she looked—but wasn't that one of her habitual expressions? That she had been deeply fond of Pinka when Pinka was alive there could be no doubt. But what she felt now was inscrutable. It was possible, Leonard thought, that she had forgotten Pinka ever existed. There had been no way to tell whether she missed Pinka while they were away. And now, if she was in fact mourning, she was doing so in as restrained and private a manner as the Woolfs themselves could only have admired.

One very hot afternoon toward the end of June, Mitz found herself alone in the flat. Leonard and Virginia had gone off together after lunch. Mitz had wanted to go, too, but Leonard had gently peeled her from his neck and put her on the floor. She had followed him to the door, but he had closed it on her. What was up? Usually she got to go everywhere. She did not have time to wonder: as soon as she was alone she hopped onto the windowsill, and immediately she began to drowse—an effect of the intense sunlight that was at that moment beating down. She fell asleep, suspended in that bright warmth as in a giant palm.

She woke when she heard the key in the lock. Ah, here they were home again—now she might get something to eat. Often when Leonard had been out he would return with a treat in his pocket: a nice warm bird's egg, a live grasshopper. Mitz yawned and jumped to the floor. The door opened, and there came into the room a perfect stranger. It was as if a cloud had blotted out the sun. Mitz went cold all over. Now Leonard and Virginia had come in too, but Mitz paid them no attention. She kept her unblinking eyes on the stranger, who was walking in circles about the room, sniffing at everything. When it caught Mitz's scent, it came flopping over, shattering the air with its cries. Deafened, furious, Mitz arched her back. She knew just what was coming, and she braced herself. Her white tufts stood on end. She flattened her ears and dropped her jaw. And when the round black wet snuffling thing drew near, she attacked.

Such a fuss! Leonard had quite a time getting the stranger calm again. Meanwhile Mitz had crossed the room in two bounds and leapt onto Leonard's shoulder. She could make noise too, you know.

"Lord!" cried Virginia, covering her ears with her hands.

Leonard shrugged, forcing Mitz to grab hold of his shirt collar or lose her balance. He raised his voice above the din. "I told you: just because she liked one dog doesn't mean she likes them all."

As Virginia went to put the kettle on, Leonard said, "Why don't we all go for a walk after tea?"

And that is what they did. They went to the square, and they chatted with the square keeper, and by that evening all Bloomsbury knew about the Woolfs' new spaniel.

"A curious case of hopeless erotic mania," was how Virginia described the new dog's feeling for Leonard. Her name was Sally. Thirteen months old, black and white, fine eyes, fine muzzle, fine head. "Very distinguished looking" but "has she intelligence?" They had got her not from Vita but from a breeder in Ickenham. And how did she compare with Pinka? "Lighter, more nervous, perhaps less solid a character than Pinka."

But what was it about Leonard that so inflamed the passions of the brute creation? Sally clung to him, and for months she would not walk with Virginia alone. As for Sally's relationship with Mitz: the two animals learned quickly to tolerate each other, but they were not friends. Though Mitz did sometimes groom Sally, she did so only lackadaisically, never with the kind of fierce concentration she devoted to Leonard's or to Pinka's hair. Again Leonard said: Give them time. But, observing Mitz's coolness toward Sally and how, even on the chilliest nights, she did not seek refuge in that black-and-white fur, Virginia felt a pang. It was silly—too silly even to voice; but she couldn't help thinking that Mitz was more faithful to Pinka than they were.

The Woolfs moved to Rodmell in midsummer. One August night, after they had gone to bed, Mitz discovered that someone had left the back door open. She sat on the doorstep, her heart wild. The world beckoned. Out she went, moving swiftly over the ground, where she did not feel safe at all, until she reached the great fig tree. In a flash she had scaled it. A breeze tossed the tree-top, and from time to time a bigger breeze blew from a different direction and rocked the whole tree. Mitz clung to her branch and was tossed and rocked. She breathed the rich smells that had baked in the earth all the hot long day and were now being released. She heard the owl and the cuckoo. The moon brightened. The statues in the garden gleamed. Shadows flocked to the orchard. Mitz feasted on insects caught on the wing. The moon paled. A fox lapped at the lily pond. The moist night air, the rustling trees, the fur-ruffling wind, the fox, the moon—oh, who can say what fears or what delights, what memories or what yearnings all this woke in tiny Mitz?

"Thank heaven!" It was morning. Virginia and Leonard stood in their nightclothes under the fig tree.

"Why can't people be more careful?" Leonard was cross. Someone had blundered.

"It must have been Janie who left the door open." (Jane Bussy, a friend who sometimes taught Virginia French, had visited the day before.) "Shall I get the net?"

"No. I'll just put my arms around you and—"

"Oh, Mitz!"

For there she was.

9

There has been much disagreement as to when Bloomsbury came into being (with some members of the group insisting that it never came into being at all). Was it in 1904, somewhere between 1912 and 1914, in 1920? Whenever Bloomsbury may truly have begun, there can be no disputing the fact that by the time Mitz arrived it was soon to end. (Leonard, looking back one day, would date the beginning of the end to the death of Lytton Strachey, in 1932.) But these twilight years were anything but dim. A world in decline it might be; it was still a world in which you could hear Eliot, Forster, and Virginia Woolf discussing James Joyce.

From Leonard's shoulder or from inside his waistcoat, Mitz peered—up or down as the case might be—into some of the most celebrated faces of the day—from the supremely lovely one of Lady Diana Cooper to the dignified one of Jawaharlal Nehru to the ratlike one of Somerset Maugham. Mitz was a witness to the stuttered excitement of Maynard Keynes announcing that he was writing a book that could change economics forever. At Monk's House and at Tavistock Square, the conversations that had begun at 46 Gordon Square three decades before were still going on—about beauty and goodness, truth and reality, art and friendship, religion and love. Opinions deemed humbug or poppycock were denounced with the same old force and disdain. Was a certain novel good or bad, was so-and-so a good or a bad painter, what can poetry do that fiction cannot and vice versa—these were the sorts of questions that were debated over crumpets and honey or roasted grouse. Which was the greater evil—to betray one's country or one's friend? Could war ever be justified? Should an artist undergo psychoanalysis? (The Woolfs published Freud.) What was the right way to take criticism? Did it matter if one was not read by the young? Why no women on the London Library Committee? (A debate that left Virginia fuming and determined to vent herself in a book called *On Being Despised.*) Could literature be taught? Should a writer accept honors? (No, said Virginia, most emphatically. She herself refused the offer of a Companion of Honour, and when asked to replace H. G. Wells as president of PEN, she exploded: "Conceive the damned insolence! Ten dinners a year, and I to sit at the head of this puling company of back scratchers and administer balm.")

There were times when Mitz, hearing particularly lively talk coming from Virginia's studio or sitting room, was baffled upon entering to find no one but Virginia herself.

And here was another mystery of Bloomsbury: people were called one name when they were present and other names when they were not. The "uncastrated cat" coming to dinner was in fact Ethel; the "great toad" and the "dear old ass" both turned out to be Tom. And who were Mr. Bennett and Mrs. Brown? Mitz heard these two mentioned often, but they never came.

Mitz was a witness also to those famous scenes when the agnostic Virginia argued with the Anglo-Catholic convert Tom about religion ("Humbug!") and the existence of God ("Poppycock!"). On these occasions Virginia could get herself quite worked up, but Tom remained calm, looking at her with the same expression as he had Mitz the time she bit him.

There were plenty of scenes between the Woolfs as well. Leonard almost never lost his temper completely, but at any sign of anger on his part, first Pinka and later Sally would slink out of the room on dachshund's legs. Not Mitz. Something about the pitch of Leonard's voice in a rage seemed to stimulate her. She hopped up and down, jabbering her two cents' worth—you would have thought she was egging him on. The Woolfs' quarrels almost all had the same source: Virginia refused to leave a party early or take proper rest or drink her milk or eat. (Of all things strange about humans to Mitz this was the strangest: how Virginia would not eat.) There were quarrels between Leonard and Mabel which inevitably bred quarrels between the Woolfs, with Virginia accusing Leonard of "making Mabel a peg on which to hang his misery." And there were Leonard's legendary quarrels with the employees of the Press. With his staff Leonard was almost as bad as he was with servants. No one could do his or her job to Leonard's satisfaction; no one knew better how a thing ought to be done than Leonard himself; he was surrounded by boobies and cheats. (Not for nothing did John Lehmann call his memoir of his years working at Hogarth *Thrown to the Woolfs*.)

Mitz happened to arrive at a turning point for the Woolfs, when the burdens of being publishers had become greater than the pleasures. First of all they did not like the way the Press tied them down. Say they wanted to go abroad for a year or so: they could not. And how weary they were of reading all those manuscripts, almost all of them bad, some "of such sublime craziness or profound stupidity," according to Leonard, "we seriously considered starting a 'Hogarth Worst Books of the Year Series.'" Mitz observed them of an evening, Leonard in his chair and Virginia in hers, turning pages, slowly at first, then faster and faster. From time to time one or the other would cry out loud—*Absolute rubbish!—Utterly insane!—To the WC!*—and hurl the pages across the room. Mitz thought they had at last found themselves a game.

On Leonard's shoulder Mitz attended meetings of the Bloomsbury Memoir Club, where Virginia took up the question "Am I a Snob?", and Maynard recalled the Cambridge of his youth, his youthful beliefs, and the influence on early Bloomsbury of the philosopher G. E. Moore. She attended countless political meetings as well. From Leonard's bosom she looked out upon various crowded rooms and halls as he participated in round tables and delivered speeches. She heard the virtues of socialism extolled, the evils of fascism and communism deplored, arguments for saving the League of Nations, proposals for the prevention of war. *War*—she heard this word repeated often, by Leonard and by others, and *Hitler* and *Germany* and *war* again. *War, war, war*—like Sally barking. And whatever it was all about, Mitz knew it was something immense, causing Leonard's heart to

race, the veins in his neck to bulge and throb, his voice
to quiver, and his hands to shake uncontrollably.

The doors of society were open to Mitz. Ottoline and
Sibyl, the two great hostesses of the day, received her into
their salons. Mitz was a guest at Garsington, where poets
and politicians strutted with the peacocks. At Argyll
House she was privy to the choicest gossip and would
hear all about Mrs. Simpson long before the scandal
made the newspapers. To Kent Mitz went for weekends at
Sissinghurst, which Vita had bought only recently and
where she was planting the first seeds of what would
become the renowned garden. There were weeks during
the London season when Mitz went out almost every
night. And though a party always excited her, and she
enjoyed the faces and the laughter and the talk—not to
mention the tidbits Leonard passed her—in this too she
was like Virginia: she could take only so much. Too many
soirées frayed her nerves and gave her a headache, and
no matter how much fun she'd had she was always glad
to be home, for really there was nothing dearer to her
than those simple book-filled rooms, her own cozy birdcage, her own fire.

The end of summer 1935 brought a sad parting: the
Woolfs' nephew, Julian Bell, left for China. He had taken
an English professorship at the National University of
Wuhan. Why? Virginia wanted to know. (In her opinion
literature could *not* be taught.) And why must he go so
far away? His mother was inconsolable. Julian was
Vanessa's eldest child and her favorite.

A few weeks earlier, having just learned that his appli-
cation for the teaching position had been accepted,

Julian had arrived at Tavistock Square, bursting with his news. As it happened, Leonard and Mitz were dining out that evening. Nephew and aunt talked a long time, in an intimate way that was not usual for them. Julian stayed till one in the morning, and the next day, writing in her diary, Virginia's mind flew ahead and she saw him returning from China "a full grown mature man, with a place in the world. He wants to write on politics & philosophy & to enter politics seriously." Then her mind flew back, to a dinner party one spring evening the year before. Tom's book *After Strange Gods* had just been published, and he and Maynard were discussing it. Julian arrived just as Maynard was railing against the younger generation: The young had no traditions, no religion. They had no discipline and no morality. Tom agreed. And the young were in too much of a hurry to publish; they could not imagine taking years and years over a book. . . . All of which might be true, young outnumbered Julian said; just the same he would rather be of his generation than of theirs. Cool. Honest. Aunt and nephew had their differences (she was hard on his poetry and his table manners, he teased her mercilessly and accused her of being cruel), but there was great affection between them. Julian had brought his mother the most extraordinary happiness; for this alone Virginia would have loved him.

It was uncertain how long Julian would remain in China—perhaps as long as three years. When he returned, Virginia mused, "He [would] be thirty & I 56 alas."

10

On the fourth of September, 1935, Virginia decided that she would call her novel *The Years*. At last she was sure of its title; now all she had to do was rewrite it. On the twenty-ninth of December she recorded in her diary that she had just written the last lines. To celebrate she lit up a cheroot and blew a fat halo into the air. It wobbled directly above Mitz's head, and when she leapt up to catch it Virginia laughed.

That was the last time Mitz would hear Virginia laugh for a long while.

The year 1936 began badly, with Virginia in bed for three days with a headache. Worse was to come. All that year she would teeter on the brink of what she called "a smash up." Months passed, and *The Years* was not finished. Virginia kept setting new deadlines for herself—end of February, tenth of March, end of August—and failing to meet them. Pages were sent to the printer and put into galleys, and when the galleys came back Virginia revised them.

But how could she publish such "feeble twaddle"? It could only bring her dishonor, she said. Her friends would be ashamed for her, and her enemies would gloat. And now she began to fear the worst: she had lost her gift; she did not know how to write anymore. She *was* "a ravaged sensitive old hack"; after all, Leonard had not been able to save her.

"I wonder if anyone has ever suffered so much from a book." Now every morning's work was a torment. Not even her beloved walks brought relief. She lost her way in familiar streets and began talking to herself. She imagined that people *knew* and were jeering at her. The sun picked her out like a searchlight. She heard the rooks crying, *Fraud! Fraud!*

Mitz could hardly fail to notice what a change had come over the household. It was as if an invisible but dangerous animal had moved in with them. No more was the sound of pen moving across paper a comforting one. How alarming now was all that hectic scribbling, that furious slashing and scratching, pages crumpled into balls, pages ripped into shreds—was a book being created or being destroyed?

Mitz could not remember the last time Virginia had sat talking to her or staring into her eyes. Even when Mitz was right under her nose, Virginia seemed not to see her. She seemed to be having trouble seeing in general: she walked into doors, she tripped over furniture. In such a situation it is the instinct of a dog to lie low. But Mitz was not Sally. As many times as Virginia shooed her away she returned—until she got the shock of her life. The kick sent her somersaulting backward across the room. When she had got her breath back, she went straight to Leonard. Virginia apologized with tears in her eyes, but after this Mitz kept her distance.

From a distance, then, Mitz observed Virginia. And she saw how this mysterious activity that could bring such a flush to Virginia's cheek could also have quite the opposite effect: Virginia was as white as her own writing paper. She scribbled and slashed; she muttered and she groaned and she cursed. She jumped up from her chair and wandered in circles about the room. She stopped before the mirror, her eyes raking her reflection. *I am old*, Mitz heard her say. *I am ugly.* To Leonard she insisted: *I am a failure.* She had lost her art and she had no children. Vanessa had both. *I have neither.*

Nineteen thirty-six. Kipling and King George died early in the year, and, later, A. E. Housman and G. K. Chesterton. The news on the wireless each night was grim. The Italians crushed Abyssinia. Hitler marched his troops into the Rhineland. There was civil war in Spain.

Staggering to the lunch table, Virginia sat down across from Leonard and refused to eat. At night she hardly slept. Leonard called in the doctors, whom Virginia loathed. Chloral, rest, and a change of scene were prescribed. And so that spring the Woolfs took a short holiday in Cornwall, and that summer they retreated for longer than usual to Monk's House. But *The Years* remained unfinished, and Virginia remained unwell. At last there came a time when she could do nothing but lie in bed, boring her way through thick volumes of Flaubert and Macaulay: the reading cure. She passed much of the summer in this way, but in autumn when they returned to London, she took up *The Years* once more.

One day in early November Virginia read the novel from the beginning and made up her mind. "I must carry the proofs, like a dead cat, to L. & tell him to burn them unread."

Leonard persuaded her to let him read the book before they destroyed it.

That evening Leonard sat down in his chair with the proofs on his lap and Mitz on his shoulder. "It was an uncertain spring." Mitz yawned, then shut her eyes tightly and slept. Sally lay in her basket, and Virginia sat slumped in her own chair in a kind of stupor of despair, awaiting her fate.

Reading *The Years* for the first time, Leonard saw that, as usual, Virginia had exaggerated. There was no reason to burn the book, no reason why it should not be published. Friends would find no cause for shame here, enemies no cause to gloat. But though she exaggerated, Leonard saw that Virginia was not wrong: *The Years* was not a masterpiece. It was not the equal of her other books. Leonard was quite sure of his judgment. The question was, what to say? He had always been honest before.

He stole a glance at Virginia, who had fallen into a doze. Caressed by soft lamplight, her face relaxed, she looked much younger than her fifty-four years, and Leonard was taken back—years back—to the first time he had ever seen her. Cambridge: Virginia and Vanessa had come to visit their brother, Leonard's friend, Thoby Stephen. Virginia was eighteen years old. She and Vanessa were dressed alike in long white dresses and summer hats, they were twirling white parasols, and their loveliness—Leonard had never seen women so lovely— took his breath away. Eleven years later, returning to England after seven years in Ceylon, he discovered that much had changed. Poor Thoby had died, of typhoid fever. Vanessa had married Clive Bell, another of Thoby's Cambridge friends, and borne two sons. Virginia had received several proposals of marriage, including one from Leonard's best friend from Cambridge days, Lytton Strachey. One thing had not changed: she was as beautiful as ever. Leonard fell in love—and just as Virginia was, at this moment, that beautiful young woman of 1912 again, Leonard was again that ardent young man who declared, "It would be worth the risk of everything to marry you."

Oh, the years indeed. Thoby dead, and Lytton dead, and Clive and Vanessa long since separated, and their two little boys grown men. Leonard sighed. Virginia was right: he doubted whether any writer had ever suffered more than she had suffered writing this book. And he to add to that suffering? No, no. Not by a jot. He could not, he must not. He must not feed her deepest fear.

He cleared his throat, loudly, bringing all three—marmoset, spaniel, wife—out of their dozes. Virginia turned to him with a look he knew well: at once fearful and trusting. Her fate was in his hands, and they both knew that. Whatever he said, she would believe him. Whatever he decided, she would accept. He cleared his throat again, and began. He had not finished the whole book, but so far—

Mitz felt the heat rising to the surface of Leonard's skin, the tension in his muscles, the pulse quickening in his neck—all signs that Leonard lied. Virginia was so agitated—her own pulse was so loud in her ears—she could hardly hear. She thought she heard the words "extraordinarily good." She *did* hear them. And at these words: "I woke from death . . . to life!"

On the last day of 1936, *The Years* went off to the printer, to be happily forgotten until spring.

*   *   *

Publication of *The Years* was set for the ides of March, and as "the fatal day" approached, Virginia went through the usual agonies, imagining herself turned, as of that day, into "the doomed discarded ridiculed novelist." But— "Oh the relief!"—the book was reviewed with the highest praise. It outsold all her other books, and in America, where it was published a month later and praised by Faulkner, it rose to the top of the fiction bestseller list.

"Money is assured," she exulted in her diary; "L. shall have his new car."

To escape the Coronation celebrations that May, the Woolfs went to France. Sally had to stay behind with Percy. Mitz, as usual, got to go along. (*Oh—un petit singe. Est-ce qu'il est dangereux?*) In one village a little girl caught snails for Mitz, who cracked them open just like the birds' eggs she had such a passion for and that Leonard and Virginia would steal for her from nests when they went walking. As for the Woolfs, at every meal they were happily indulging their own passion, for pâté de foie gras. They visited the Château de Nohant and gawked at Chopin's piano and George Sand's pens. They fell in love with the beautiful, unspoiled Dordogne and even talked about buying a house there. All in all it was a perfect holiday, and they returned to England rested and cheerful.

But all the happiness of that spring was darkened by a shadow, and that shadow was cast by Julian. He had returned from China—changed, as might have been expected, but not quite in the expected way. Everyone saw that he was now a more solemn and serious character. He was also unhappy. He was bitter. What had his brilliant Bloomsbury upbringing prepared him for? he demanded with a sneer. Certainly not for any profession.

He had resigned his teaching position and to everyone's dismay announced that he was going to fight for the republic in Spain. Vanessa was beside herself.

Two days before Julian left for Spain, there was a farewell dinner at his father's house, in Gordon Square. Though he could not be dissuaded from his plan, Julian had made this concession: he would offer himself not as a soldier but as an ambulance driver. Now Clive and Leonard agreed that he probably would be in no more danger than he would be at home, driving between London and Charleston. Virginia was outraged. Oh, the stupidity of men! No wonder there were wars. She and Vanessa knew— But no, she must not let her mind run to that. Indeed, she must keep her mind off worrying about Julian, and as always the most distracting activity was work.

Already Virginia had begun *Three Guineas*, the political pamphlet she had been itching to write for some time and which she had once thought of calling *On Being Despised*. It had begun as a sequel to *A Room of One's Own*, the pamphlet she had published in 1929 and in which she discussed the fate of the woman writer in a patriarchal world. In the sequel she planned to discuss education and professions for women. But now, with the threat of fascism and war always present, she began thinking of it also as her "war pamphlet": a meditation upon the reasons for war and what might be done to prevent it. Virginia believed that fascism, the pursuit of war, and the oppression of women were all connected, and in *Three Guineas* she meant to show how.

The book was coming along smoothly—a great relief after the ordeal of *The Years*. And there were other distractions. Earlier that year, in April, the Woolfs had taken

Sally back to the breeder in Ickenham, to be mated. Now they were in suspense: was she pregnant or did she just have worms?

In June Leonard bought a family of three tortoises for the pond at Monk's House. They turned out to be unexpectedly lively. One in particular seemed bent on escape, and on certain days of that summer of 1937 this astonishing sight could be seen: Virginia Woolf, hitching up her skirts and lolloping down the road in pursuit of the father.

A cry rang out in Fitzroy Street.

It was a cry of such anguish and such force that those who heard it stopped whatever they were doing and stood still. Hands involuntarily flew to throats, blood drained from cheeks, knees shook.

Vanessa lay on her back on her bed, her limbs splayed, her head twisted at an unlikely angle. A body flung from the roof would have landed so, every bone shattered. Her eyes rolled, her jaw worked, her bosom rose and fell. And Virginia saw that "the death of a child is childbirth again."

Now one could say it: they both had known Julian would die in Spain. He had survived there less than two months.

Vanessa said, "I thought when Roger died that I was unhappy."

Roger, and Lytton, and their brother Thoby, whom Julian so much resembled and who, like Julian, had died in his youth—oh, the people they had buried! Vanessa lay on her bed, and Virginia sat beside her, and they remembered and they wept. They had been just girls when their mother died, suddenly. And then, only two years later, their beloved half-sister Stella, who had taken their mother's place, died suddenly, too. Their father died—not suddenly, he, but horribly slowly—when the Stephen sisters were in their early twenties. (Not for nothing did Henry James once call the Stephen house "that house of all the Deaths.")

Virginia went to her sister every day ("the only point in the day one could want to come," Vanessa told Vita.) Almost at once she sat down and wrote a short memoir of Julian. When she was not at her sister's side, Virginia was working. (Work: that great solace and distraction; everyone knew that the turning point for Vanessa would be when she started painting again.) Mourning Julian, Virginia reminded herself that he had died for a noble cause; it had been a gallant death, hadn't it? But no, she could not hold on to this consolation. *Why had he done it? Why had he gone to Spain?* It was an agony to try to reconstruct what had happened, from the various conflicting accounts that came to them over the following weeks. The bomb hitting the ambulance. The shrapnel piercing his chest. How another man who was with him had survived without a scratch. Waiting for surgery, he had asked what his chances were and been told a lie. It was a miracle and not an operation he needed. In the end for some reason he spoke in French. He died that same night. He was twenty-nine.

Later that summer, when Virginia went on her walks, Julian began to appear to her: a large man, carelessly dressed as always, in a floppy hat and torn trousers, speaking and gesturing quickly, as was his way. He appeared at her side, and she found herself arguing with him, as they walked, and she found *Three Guineas* turning into this: an argument with Julian, about war. "We have to choose war, not peace," he had written in one of his essays. *What did he mean?* Love of war was incomprehensible to Virginia, as she thought it must be to all women. Try as she would, she could make no sense of Julian's desire to go to Spain. She could not escape the idea that his death had been a "complete waste." And there was a part of her—she could not help it—that would never forgive him for going to war, for dying, for poisoning all their hard-earned happiness, for devastating his mother. Vanessa said, "I shall be cheerful, but I shall never be happy again." Had he not foreseen this? Yes, Virginia was sure he had, for they had loved each other passionately, mother and son. Still, he had gone. And now Virginia was reminded of Lytton's words, a phrase that appeared near the end of *Queen Victoria*: "some monstrous reversal of the course of nature." Yes, so it seemed: as if some monstrous reversal of the course of nature had occurred: the child dying while the mother lived on.

But day by day Vanessa improved. Virginia charted her progress hopefully in letters and in her diary. One day Nessa sat up in bed and ate something. One day she smiled. At last one night she was able to sleep without a sleeping draught. She did a little embroidery. She answered condolence letters. "Next week I expect Nessa will begin painting." By mid-August she was up and about and walking in the garden at Charleston. On the ninth of September she wrote to her sister not to come see her if it was too much trouble: "I really need not be visited like an invalid now." And a few weeks later came this most promising sign: Vanessa took a trip with her family to Paris, to see an exhibition of French masterpieces.

A busy season for the Woolfs began. Sally got a thorn, and her paw swelled up "as big as a soup plate," according to Virginia (no doubt exaggerating again). They got the thorn out with a poultice. ("Now if only we could poultice *your* thorns," Leonard teased Virginia.) This medical emergency was hardly dealt with when another arose. One of Mitz's canines was loose—most likely from decay. (All that honey and tapioca?) The tooth could not be ignored, for it interfered with Mitz's two favorite activities: eating and grooming.

Virginia held her breath as Leonard cradled the tiny head in his palm and extracted the tooth with trembling fingers. And she felt a new respect for Mitz—for being clever enough to understand that Leonard was trying to help her, and for bearing up so stoically through what could not have been a painless procedure. (When Virginia herself had had two teeth out some years before, she had been liberally dosed with cocaine.)

After Mitz's gum had stopped bleeding, Leonard rewarded her with a macaroon. "I'm afraid she's getting old," he said. How old she was, of course, they did not know. But Leonard remembered what he had been told by the keeper at the London Zoo: how they had never been able to keep a marmoset alive there for more than four years. The Woolfs had had Mitz for about four years now.

They saved the tooth: a long yellow splinter with a fine gray line running through it. "Lose another, Mitzi," Virginia said, "and I'll have a pair of earrings."

On the twelfth of October Virginia finished a draft of *Three Guineas* and began to revise it.

Worms indeed had turned out to be the disappointing cause of Sally's tumid condition, and in December the Woolfs took her back to Ickenham to be mated again.

For Christmas that year Vita sent a magnificent Strasbourg pie ("what immortal geese must have gone to make it!") which the Woolfs shared with Tom. "Complete silence reigned. The poet ate; the novelist ate; Even Leonard, who had a chill inside, ate."

The Keyneses came to Monk's House on Christmas Day. Maynard had not quite recovered from a bad heart attack he had suffered in May, and when the talk turned, as it always did, to politics, and he, as always, grew agitated, Lydia wisely whisked him away.

All that year Leonard's health, too, had given cause for worry. There had been several scares. Diabetes was suspected; then prostate, then kidneys. There had been countless visits to specialists; there had been examinations and tests.

Now, with the beginning of a new year came a new scare.

Leonard lay in bed, pale, feverish. He had been reading the newspaper, but now his eyes were closed and he seemed to be drowsing. Mitz lay curled on the pillow by his head, and Sally slept at his feet. Sitting nearby, pretending to read but in fact watching anxiously, Virginia felt a burning pressure building behind her nose. She could not bear to think of the possibility—and yet it was all too real, that possibility—for see how unwell he was, he had never been so unwell, and the doctors were puzzled and did not even try to hide their concern. There was talk of admitting him to a nursing home for observation; there was talk of surgery. Meanwhile a regimen of rest and rice pudding had been prescribed—and appeared to be doing precisely nothing.

Without Leonard life would have no meaning at all. The years had taught Virginia this. The happy years, the many years (they had celebrated their silver anniversary that August). And they had not grown apart, as couples do: they were closer than they had ever been. Only that autumn Virginia had decided she wanted to go to Paris. Vanessa was there, Vita was there, Virginia knew of a certain small hotel—it would be such fun. But then Leonard announced that he wasn't up to the trip; if Virginia wanted to go, she should go alone. And why not? she thought—but then it struck her: A holiday without Leonard? What would be the point? Without Leonard, it would not be a holiday at all. And oh, what heaves and swells of love had accompanied this revelation. All her desire to go to Paris dissolved. To be separated even for days would be unbearable. To be separated— To be without— Alone—

And here Virginia could no longer prevent it: she began to cry.

Leonard opened his eyes, looked round the room in confusion for a moment, and closed them again. Behind his lids his eyes rolled upward. Lord, he felt wretched! Now Sally, upset by Virginia's sobs, began to whine. She clambered up over Leonard, crumpling the newspaper. This in turn woke Mitz, who sat up and began her excited chattering. For some reason this made Virginia cry harder, and then Sally barked, and Mitz in a frenzy threw herself at Leonard's head and bit his ear, and Leonard lost his temper.

"Sally, *down!*" he shouted, at the same time batting

Mitz away from him. "If you don't *mind,* I'm *supposed* to be getting my *rest!*" And with a grimace—for he really was in pain—he rolled over onto his side, turning his back to Virginia.

Virginia wiped her nose and said in a voice so small she might have been addressing a mouse, "Oh, Leonard. What would we do without you?"

Leonard groaned. "Don't worry," he said. "I'll live." There was silence then. The animals had settled back down. After a few minutes Virginia thought Leonard had fallen asleep. But he spoke again, in the soft mumbling voice of one on the verge of sleep: "Don't worry, ladies, I'll live. You'll see. I'll outlive you all."

12

By the end of January Leonard was back on his feet; his specimens began showing up normal, and whatever the danger had been (and they would never know exactly), it was past. After weeks of nothing but rice pudding, Leonard attacked his meals as voraciously as Mitz did hers. And for once Virginia did not mind. He could have licked his plate—he could have got down on all fours and fought Sally for her bone—and Virginia would have cheered.

On the third of February, Virginia wrote to Vanessa: "You know I'd do anything I could to help you, and its so awful not to be able to: except to adore you as I do." It was the eve of Julian's birthday. A ghost that could not be laid to rest, a death she could not fit in anywhere—so her nephew continued to haunt Virginia. Had they done something wrong? she kept asking herself. Was it something in Bloomsbury's teaching that had driven him to go and get himself killed? Once, she had imagined him coming home from China a grown man with a place in the world; now that place was nothing but a black hole. And in Spain, day by day, the cause that had drunk his blood was being lost.

Spring came, and Virginia's heart was raked anew: "Why is he not here to see the daffodils; the old beggar woman—the swans . . ."

After endless deliberation, the Woolfs agreed to sell half the Press—Virginia's half—to their former assistant John Lehmann, who would take over as manager the following autumn.

With *Three Guineas* behind her, Virginia began writing *Roger Fry*. Leonard was writing something he had long been pondering: *The Hotel*, a play about the end of European civilization.

One morning while she was working in her studio in the basement of Tavistock Square, Virginia put down her pen, aware of a faint vibration, as of some deep nerve plucked. She leaned forward; she held her breath. The eerie and rapturous feeling that something was about to be communicated to her, as from another world. She half closed her eyes and she waited. What came: a muffled music, like distant horns; a soft rising and falling, a rhythm to which she matched her breathing when she breathed again. Looking round her studio, she saw a kind of haze over all—and the next instant her mind took flight: people, houses, streets, landscapes, weather, seasons, friendships, passions, fates, patterns, necessities—

A new novel.

In April Ottoline Morell died. For Virginia "a queer

loveliness departed." In an obituary for *The Times*, she remembered (surely not without a pang) how her dear old flamboyant friend had not "escape[d] the ridicule of those whom she befriended."

Their friends were dying. They were getting old. ("L. says we are old. I say we are middle aged.") Even the goddess: Vanessa would be fifty-nine that May. Mitz was not the only one to observe how, as they grew older, the Woolfs were beginning to look more and more alike— the same long gaunt serious faces; brother and sister some people mistook them for at first—and now, what with all her scribbling, Virginia too had developed a tremor of the hands.

The publication of *Three Guineas* in June brought considerable disappointment. Neither Leonard nor Vanessa found much to like in the book. Maynard hated it. Vita found it full of "misleading arguments," and she and Virginia quarreled over it. Reviews were the anticipated "sneer enthusiasm, enthusiasm sneer." But *Three Guineas* was nonfiction, and Virginia was not nearly as sensitive about her nonfiction as she was about her fiction. Besides, though shop owners had predicted it would not, *Three Guineas* was selling. Furthermore, Virginia was now thoroughly absorbed in writing her two new books: *Roger Fry* and *Pointz Hall*, the book that would in time become *Between the Acts*, her last novel. In the end the publication of *Three Guineas* seemed to Virginia her "mildest childbirth" yet.

For that year's holiday the Woolfs chose Scotland. They were gone for the last two weeks of June, and this time both Mitz and Sally went along.

A pilgrimage to the bonnie blue lochs and purple hills of Scott country. They visited Melrose and the ruins of

Dryburgh Abbey, where the syringa bloomed round the great man's tomb. As usual on holiday, they ate well, especially at breakfast. Oh, the porridge! Oh, the creamed haddock and the heavenly shortbread!

Mitz drew the usual gawking crowds, and Sally got ticks, which Mitz, that champion nitpicker, left Leonard to deal with. The Woolfs met a couple who had friends who had actually seen the Loch Ness monster, and so they got a vivid if secondhand account of that headless creature ripping through the water "like several broken telegraph posts." On the Isle of Skye they stayed at a famous hotel (Boswell and Johnson had slept there). All this Virginia reported faithfully in letters back home— but did Vanessa believe her when she wrote that, on Skye, "the old women live in round huts exactly the shape of skye terriers"?

It had been "the worst spring on record," according to Virginia. Now it was the "worst July on record." Some allowance perhaps should be made for her habit of exaggeration, but certainly the drought that year was very bad, withering crops and foliage and even parching the pipes of church organs.

Monk's House that summer was filled with workmen. The Woolfs were having a new room built. This would be Leonard's library and promised to be quite cozy, tucked under the roof, with a fireplace. It was Leonard's idea that they should turn one end of the new room into a veranda, where they saw themselves cooling off on hot nights, smoking and stargazing.

In spite of the chaos, the Woolfs worked every day as usual, but Mitz was so unstrung by all the hammering she spent most of her time under a pillow. At the end of August the Woolfs tried again to have Sally mated—again without success. (It was love of Leonard, a frustrated Virginia had taken to saying, that had made the bitch barren.)

The Woolfs had planned to stay in Rodmell until well into October. But on the twenty-sixth of September they were abruptly called back to London.

The thing most feared was happening. Most feared but hardly unexpected. It had been gathering for weeks, that darkness. No: it had been gathering much longer— months, years.

That March Hitler had invaded Austria, and Virginia had predicted: "When the tiger . . . has digested his dinner he will pounce again." Now he crouched at the border of Czechoslovakia. *Gross-Deutschland*, he growled.

Driving back to London, although they were not going fast (it was raining), to Leonard it seemed as if they were hurtling downhill at incredible speed, heading straight for a pit. His fingers gripped the steering wheel so hard that they ached. It was chilly in the car. Sally's breath befogged the glass. Leonard had wrapped Mitz in a scarf and tucked her into one of his coat pockets; it seemed to him that the cold was bothering her more and more these days.

Eyes fixed on the road, brow furled and lips compressed, Leonard presented a grim profile to Virginia. And among all the other emotions flooding her at that moment was a swell of pity for Leonard: the crisis had plunged him into a despair even darker than her own. How many hours of his life had been devoted to averting the very cataclysm that now threatened them. The endless meetings and committees, the speeches, the petitions, the pamphlets, and the articles—all had failed.

Up until now, even with planes roaring over the downs

and Hitler roaring over the wireless during the Nuremberg rally, the Woolfs had managed to work. But now they could think of nothing but war. Never had they felt so helpless, and helplessness, they were discovering, was exhausting. So the hare goes limp in the falcon's claws. . . . Virginia had a great longing to be near her sister, but the Bells had gone to stay for two months in Cassis.

Looking out through the rain, Virginia thought of her family, her friends, her houses, her books. Would she live to write another book? In such dark times it was a blessing to be childless. Vanessa had lost one son already. Would she now lose the other?

Here Mitz, tucked in Leonard's pocket, began to fret, and he reached in a hand to comfort her.

Did we tell you how the marmoset saved us from Hitler?

War. Would they survive? Would there be anything left worth surviving for?

It is the worst that could happen to us, Virginia thought, for once not exaggerating at all.

13

In London trenches were being dug in the parks, and sandbags were being piled up, and shopkeepers were boarding up their windows. Government cars prowled the streets with megaphones warning everyone to get fitted for a gas mask.

As soon as they arrived at Tavistock Square, Leonard and Mitz hastened to the office of the editor of the *New Statesman,* who had called a meeting about the crisis. Virginia went to buy coffee. Most shops and offices were open, and people were gravely going about their business; everyone seemed resigned to war.

Walking in New Oxford Street, her heart as heavy as one of the sandbags, Virginia thought: I am old. I have—what?—ten?—perhaps fifteen years remaining. Is it asking too much to be allowed to live them in peace?

The next morning the telephone rang and rang—for Leonard and for Leonard. Virginia escaped to the London Library, where she did some research for *Roger*

Fry. Afterward, at the National Gallery, she peeked in on a crowd hearing a lecture on Watteau. Wandering through the museum, gazing at Cézannes and Renoirs, she was swept by an emotion at once poignant and harrowing: she might have been saying good-bye.

The Woolfs decided to return to Rodmell that evening. The prime minister would address the House of Commons the next day. All one could do was wait, and surely it was better to wait in the country. Anyone able to leave London was being urged by the government to do so. It was believed that, at the outbreak of war, the Germans would begin by bombing London steadily three times an hour. Makeshift hospitals were being set up for miles around. There were plans to evacuate thousands of children, and, at the zoo, keepers stood ready to kill all the dangerous animals.

The drive back was hellish: pounding rain, flooded roads, jammed traffic—it took the Woolfs an hour longer than usual. Before they went to bed that night, they were visited by a civil defense officer who gave them their gas masks. (What about Mitz? What about Sally?) The next day the man was back to talk about refugees. How many of the fifty children expected to arrive in Rodmell could the Woolfs put up? Two, they said, and were told to be prepared to receive them at any time. The Woolfs shook their heads. At their age, suddenly to be parents, and of strange, frightened children—it was a daunting prospect.

That afternoon, huddled by the wireless, they heard not the expected declaration of war but the news that the prime minister was going the next day to meet Hitler in Munich.

For the next twenty-four hours the Woolfs tried to behave normally—but how could they, with their gas masks sitting on the drawing-room table, and planes roaring over the downs, and two children arriving perhaps any minute?

That night all over England was heard the same prayer. Next day came the answer: agreement reached, Hitler appeased, Czechoslovakia a small price to pay. . . . Cheers greeted the prime minister upon his return, and church bells rang out all over the empire.

Leonard called the pact a national disgrace and gave it six months. Others thought it might last a year.

Oh, what do you do at a time like this—when you are at the mercy of jousting emotions, on the one horse Shame and on the other Relief? What do you do when you know all you've got for the price of disgrace is another six months or a year?

If you are Leonard or Virginia Woolf, you throw yourself into your work.

They had their own trenches: they buried themselves in books.

These days Virginia was reading mostly memoirs (her favorite genre), mostly in French: Chateaubriand, Madame de Sévigné, Colette. And now she began thinking about writing yet another book: a history of English literature. Leonard, having finished his play about the end of European civilization, had accepted a commission from a publisher to write a book about the end of European civilization. But first he must finish volume 2 of *After the Deluge: A Study of Communal Psychology.* (Volume 1 had been published in 1931.)

Vanessa was still in Cassis—sadly for Virginia, who was never quite at ease without her sister near. Virginia herself was very fond of that part of France, and of the villa the Bells had built among the vineyards. Now was the season of the vintage, and she yearned to see with her own eyes the beauty that Vanessa described in her letters. To taste the wine, to sit on the rocks in the bay basking in the Mediterranean sun and staring at the Mediterranean blue till hypnotized— But again, she could not bear to be separated from Leonard. Going to call him in to tea one day, she saw him standing on a ladder against a tree, "where he looked so beautiful my heart stood still with pride that he ever married me."

One afternoon when Virginia was at Monk's House alone (Leonard had business in London), she looked up from her book and asked: Where's Mitz?

Gone! she shouted into the telephone. *Gone gone gone gone gone.*

Someone had blundered again, and this time it was Virginia.

She had been cooking oatcakes and burned them; to clear the smoke, she had opened the windows. But that was hours ago, she told Vanessa. By now Mitz was probably halfway to London. Virginia was sure that Mitz had gone after Leonard. Like Sally—like Virginia herself— Mitz tended to be restless when Leonard wasn't there, and was more likely to try to escape then.

Vanessa, hearing how distressed her sister was and having prayed for just this event so often, could not help feeling guilty. Had Virginia searched the house? From top to bottom, Virginia assured her—and the garden and the orchard and the churchyard, too.

And after she said good-bye to Vanessa, who after all could do little to help from France, Virginia searched again.

Outside Sally lay in the grass among the many apples a recent storm had brought down. She watched Virginia run hither and thither crying, *Mitz! Mitz!* Sally did not like Mitz—she never had. (When Virginia guessed that "being the only animal" would make Sally happier, she was absolutely correct.) And so when—not hours, as Virginia feared, but thirty minutes ago at most—Mitz had sidled past Sally and out through the gate, Sally had not tried to stop her. She had not tried to alert Virginia. She had *meant* to bark, she had even opened her mouth to bark, but somehow the bark had turned into a yawn. My, she was sleepy!

But now, waking to Virginia's frantic cries, Sally was stricken. And she seemed to hear another, deeper voice, crying, *Bad dog! Bad dog!* If it were left to Virginia, Mitz would never be found. Virginia didn't have the legs. More important, she didn't have the nose. But for Sally it was not too late. She was not a bad dog. She would redeem herself. She jumped to her feet and dashed out the gate.

"It was the most extraordinary thing," Virginia told Vanessa. "I was upstairs looking everywhere for her when I heard Sally barking. I thought someone was at the door. I went down—and there was Mitz sitting in her cage!" Virginia had stood amazed. Had Mitz been there all along? Was Virginia going mad? Inspecting Mitz, Virginia found her perfectly sound—but how had her fur got so damp?

Altogether a most extraordinary story—and one that Virginia had no intention of sharing with Leonard. And so it was his turn for bewilderment when, some time later, he heard from several people in the village that Sally had been seen racing through Rodmell with a squirrel in her mouth. Gentle Sally had never killed any creature. Isn't that strange? he said to Virginia. And Virginia, looking at Sally with new eyes, said *very.*

Now it was the middle of October, and time to move back to Bloomsbury. The Woolfs were disconcerted to see the heaps of sandbags that were still in place there. Despite Leonard's precautions, Mitz caught a chill on the drive in, and here was another anxiety. Leonard bundled her up like a refugee, and she looked so miserable, sniveling and shivering, they just wanted to give her a nice hot thimble of tea.

14

Poor Leonard! He had a terrible rash. His back looked as if he had wallowed in the raspberry patch. The doctor was scratching his head again: was it the prostate, or was it new pajamas?

Poor Virginia! She was haunted by the horrors of last January—when Leonard had been so ill and the doctors baffled and she frightened nearly out of her wits—needlessly, as it turned out. And there was something else fretting her: a new book, by Cyril Connolly, wherein she discovered that Virginia Woolf was no longer the important writer she had been a decade ago; she was out of fashion among the young; her reputation was not as high as Morgan's, not as high as Tom's. So her sore spots were rubbed as raw as Leonard's back.

Poor Mitz! She could not sit on Leonard's shoulder, because of the rash.

Poor Sally! The doctor decided *she* was to blame: Leonard must be allergic to her hair. On doctor's orders he was keeping his distance, and never was spaniel more forlorn.

But as it turned out Sally's hair might not be to blame after all. Probably it was the moth powder Mabel had sprinkled in Leonard's pajamas. *Probably trying to kill me,* Leonard grumbled. (Virginia bit her tongue.)

November brought two major events: the return of Vanessa from Cassis, and the publication by the Hogarth Press of *Julian Bell: Essays, Poems and Letters.*

It was very cold that December. Snow seeped through the skylight at Tavistock Square. The Woolfs planned to go as usual to Monk's House for Christmas and to stay there for a month. Their last guest before leaving London was Tom. They talked mostly about his new play, *The Family Reunion*—but it would not have been dinner with Old Possum without the usual grousing about the younger generation, who were turning out to be so disappointing. Even Auden. Even Isherwood. *Dis-ap-point-ing.*

It snowed the day the Woolfs left for Rodmell. At Monk's House the pipes froze and the electricity went out, so they could not cook. They would have starved had it not been for Vita's gift: an immense Strasbourg pie, just like the one she'd sent the year before. The Woolfs dined off it, meal after meal, for days.

Meanwhile the harsh weather persisted. The house was so cold they could see their breath. The windows were solid blocks of ice—it was like living in an igloo. The Woolfs bundled themselves up in coats and shawls and sat as close to the fire as they dared. They wore old pairs of gloves with the fingertips cut off to keep their hands warm while they wrote and read.

Leonard was afraid for Mitz, whom he had taken to carrying about in a tea cozy. He took her to bed with him at night, hoping that she would stay. But Mitz was a creature of habit too. She would curl up on the pillow or perch on Leonard's foot while he was awake, but as soon as he had fallen asleep, she would jump off the bed and scamper downstairs to the birdcage, where she had slept every night for the past four and a half years. She would rearrange her cloth scraps, as she always did, and when she had them close to how she wanted them (they were never perfect, of course) she would groom herself, as she did every night, combing every strand of fur through her long incisors.

It was the fifth night since the Woolfs had arrived at Monk's House. Outside, the snow was falling. The garden and the orchard lay deep in snow, snow hid the frozen lily pond, and the statues wore ermine. It was a night made for sleep. The owl did not hunt that night but slept, his beak in his breast. The fox slept in his den. Rabbits and mice slept in their holes. All Rodmell slept—village and churchyard lay sunk in sleep, the living as deep as the dead. Under many blankets and layers of clothes, Leonard and Virginia slept, in their separate rooms. Sally in her basket slept by the sleeping fire, and in her cage, curled in a damp, shivering ball, slept Mitz.

Let them sleep.

And now, while all is still and all things are sunk in snow and sleep, let us go back, to the beginning.

Forget this English village, trapped in the storm's white chrysalis, and imagine a place as unlike it as place could be. Forget white, and imagine every shade of green— yellowish, brownish, grayish, bluish, blackish—the many hues of jungle and marsh, palm frond, fern, bush, liana, creeper, and moss. Imagine this place where the light is green and the shadows are green, where wild banana plants grow, and coconut trees, and orchids whose brilliant colors—scarlet, indigo, mauve—are repeated in the wings of the butterflies. A world of damp heat and downpours, of opalescent mists and nights of thickest darkness and stillness broken at dawn by the cries of monkeys and birds. A world without houses or streets, parks or squares; without motor cars, printing presses, armchairs, beds, books, birdcages or fireplaces, inkpots or teapots, Strasbourg pies, strawberries and cream, roasted grouse, grousing poets, blizzards, ladyships, or spaniels—but not without men.

By canoe and by horseback they came, or by foot, hacking their way through the bush: men with machetes, men with nets. Different stories were passed from tree to tree about the monkeys that disappeared with them. They would be eaten, went one story. They would live happily ever after, went another: pampered and cherished, they would be carried about on the heads and shoulders of men, who only wanted them for friends.

Mitz believed the first story. She fought with all her strength when the net came down. Thrust into a saddlebag, unable to see but aware that every bouncing step was bearing her farther from home, she screamed herself hoarse. She bit and scratched at the hands that seized her (uselessly, for they were covered by thick gloves) and transferred her to a small wooden box. A panic such as she had never known came over her inside that box. Uselessly she clawed at the bottom, the sides, the top. There was not enough air—yet her lungs seemed full to bursting.

When she came to, rough hands were roughly examining her. She was given some water but nothing to eat.

How much time had passed? Hours? Days?

She was clapped into a cage, and though it was a very large cage, it was not large enough to contain all the monkeys that were crammed into it. No room to move, but move they did, jumping on top of one another, milling and shoving, in terror and confusion, shrieking, as monkeys in terror and confusion do. Looking out, Mitz saw that there were other cages just like this one, bursting with monkeys: she saw tiny marmosets like herself; she saw ringtailed monkeys and spider monkeys and squirrel monkeys. And there were cages filled with parrots, whose frightened squawking cut through even the monkeys' racket. And there were snakes, each in a cage by itself: anacondas, silent but restless, coiling, coiling. The largest cage appeared to be empty—but no: a pair of gleaming topazes hovered there, and Mitz could make out the hulking black shape of jungle royalty.

Thus it began: voyage of fear—endless dark, hunger, and thirst. The pandemonium quieted soon enough and was replaced by a deathly stillness. Now and then the sound of heavy footfall was heard, and there came into view a pair of bandy legs, a pair of tattooed arms, and a red, shiny, grimacing face.

"Faugh! What a stench!"

The lamp he held sent seasick shadows lurching through the hold.

An eye wept on his biceps, black tears spelled out *Mother.* Mother brought food, Mother brought water—but at the sound of Mother's heavy step, the parrots flapped, the monkeys cringed, the panther arched his back and growled. Mother took a knife from his belt and jabbed it through the bars, laughing. He dropped a burning ash into a begging paw. Oh, worse, far worse, was when he came staggering down with one or two mates. They roared into the cages and cracked bottles against them. They swung a tamarin round and round by its tail, then tossed it in with a snake, who spasmed once and crushed it like one of the rats that Mother usually fed it. They undid their trousers and peed on the panther.

How much time had passed? Soon enough the cages were roomy. Fevers raged. There was the constant sound of wheezing and coughing. Fur and feather alike crawled with vermin. Bodies piled up, grew hard and then soft again before they were finally removed. When Mother came down now it was with a gin-soaked bandanna pressed to his face. He carried a long stick—how else was he expected to tell living from dead?

How much time had passed? How much time remained?

[In Rodmell, it is dawn. It is still snowing. Mitz has stopped shivering at last and lies stretched out on the bottom of her cage. Lifting her head, asleep but with eyes wide open, Sally barks softly at a ghost. Leonard dreams that he is giving a speech. He clears his throat. Virginia is writing a letter to her father. She drops her pen and, bending to retrieve it, falls half out of bed, and wakes. She hears Sally barking softly at the ghost. "Gentlemen," she hears Leonard say, before falling asleep again.]

"How dainty she is!" "How grotesque!" "How adorable!" "Oh, the dirty thing—look what she's done!" "The little devil bit me!" "She looks sickly—we'll all be catching some nasty disease." "Oh, she is sweet—just like a little lady!"

When the fever broke, Mitz was alone. She was neither caged nor free. She was chained to a perch—a sturdy perch made from the thick branch of an oak tree and lately the roost of a crimson macaw. What had become of the others, the few that had survived, Mitz did not know. Toward the end it had been one long dark delirious night. The last thing she remembered (if it was not a hallucination) was watching some men struggle with the dead weight of the panther.

Now here she sits chained to a perch in a window. Someone has dressed her in bonnet and frock. Beyond the plate glass lies a bustling street. Mitz can see other windows across the way, one filled with bolts of colored fabric and another with umbrellas and another with hats—many adorned with a bright feather or two, the only thing in this new world recognizable to Mitz. Cars, vans, and omnibuses rattle past, and street hawkers roll their barrows along, shouting. Dogs bark, and now and then comes the music of an accordion or a barrel organ. A steady crowd of people tramps by, clerks and servants and shop assistants, almost all in too great haste to notice the spectacle of a marmoset dressed in Victorian doll's clothes. But then at last a head turns, steps halt, a finger points, knuckles rap on the glass (despite the clearly displayed sign asking people please not to do that). After gawking a bit, the person might move on, but often he will enter, agitating that little bell whose jingle summons one or the other or both of the owners from the depths of the shop. He is tall and stooped, with round spectacles and a sharp nose that make him look owlish. She is small and stooped and pockmarked. They are the Creaches, husband and wife.

And this is Mitz's purpose (as it was once the macaw's): to entice people into the Creaches' shop. It is for this that they have dressed her in a doll's frock and bonnet (though were she as naturally gaudy as the macaw she might have been spared this) and chained her to a perch in the window. It is their hope that, once the customer has satisfied his curiosity about Mitz (yes, she bites; no, she is not for sale), he might look about and find something else to buy in this shop overflowing with merchandise, admittedly not in the best shape, much of it, but of the most extraordinary variety. Here are horsehair sofas and chairs, tables and lamps, mirrors, sideboards, umbrella stands, sets of tarnished silver—incomplete, of course, as are the sets of china. Here are shelves piled with crockery, an entire wall of tumblers and bottles and pitchers and jars. Coins, combs, rings, buttons, medals, watches, and pins fill several glass cases. Faded carpets lie rolled up in corners, and scattered about are various old instruments: crucibles, mortars, compasses, scales. An antique microscope sits by an antique typewriter. There are weathervanes and cameras, artificial flowers, living plants. There are curiosities from the Far East—a Siamese temple gong, tiny round slippers made for bound feet—and from the Far West—a tomahawk, a bronze spittoon, a mail pouch used by the old Pony Express. Whose ancestors are these whose portraits hang crooked on the walls? Who owned these rusted rifles, and are they the rifles that brought down the beasts whose fanged and antlered heads are mounted above them? These are idle questions for the Creaches. For the Creaches the only question is who will buy.

Oh, this cold! this damp! Mitz has never known anything like it, how it sinks like icy teeth into the bones. That *jing-a-ling-ling*, which to the Creaches meant a customer and perhaps a sale, to Mitz meant a particularly nasty draft (it had been the death of the macaw). She aches all over—her joints, her back. And how to make it understood that a diet of banana, more banana, and nothing but banana was distasteful to her? (Spitting and flinging pieces about had not done the trick.) And the chain! Half the people who came into the shop *must* jerk it. And the clothes! Mitz could not move without stumbling on the hem of her skirt, and the bonnet was tied too tightly under her chin. Tugging and tugging at the knot, she flies into a rage. "Such a tongue on her!" The Creaches laugh: she must have learned to swear like that from the sailors.

(A sailor it was who had brought her to the shop, bundled in a reeking bandanna. That she was not his to sell could be seen plainly in his flushed face. That he would take anything, anything for her, so desperately dry was he—this too was plain. Why not? thought the Creaches. Put her in the window, catch people's eye, just like poor old Macawber, may he rest in peace. Wouldn't be the first stolen goods they had received, either.)

For a time it looked as if they had been cheated. They had not realized at first that Mitz was half dead. But they fed her and watered her, and she grew stronger. She chattered and swore. She threw her food about. She's fit as a fiddle now, they said. But she was not. Some days the pain was too much for her: she sat unmoving on her perch. Passersby wondered: was she stuffed? They knocked and knocked on the glass (so insistently, some, the Creaches feared it would crack; hence the sign).

Day after day Mitz sat in the window staring out at the

street: so busy; so often murky with rain or fog. No green anywhere. How was it possible for the world to have changed so completely? Looking out, Mitz saw nothing to remind her of home. But then one day—it was the hour when the lamps came on—she was astonished to see—could it really be?—the panther! Not dead after all, but walking by under her very nose. Oh, it was he all right: his black fur, his topaz eyes—but shrunk to such a puny size—why, he was hardly bigger than a spider monkey! And no one seemed to be afraid of him, no one was paying him the least attention. But wait: here was someone: an old woman carrying several parcels approached him and bowed; whereupon he dashed into the street (a bus just missing him, the woman crying out). Mitz watched him disappear into the alley next to the hat shop. So: he might not be king of this forest, but at least he was free. She had given up hope that she herself would ever be free again; that she would ever breathe sweet air, hop from branch to branch, hunting butter-flies in a land of green light and green shade. . . .

Jing-a-ling-ling! Mrs. Creach narrowed her eyes, taking the measure of the man who had just entered the shop. Not the usual customer. There was solid gold ticking in his lordship's waistcoat, a diamond in his lapel. The mar-moset? No, she didn't bite; yes, she was for sale.

A gift for the wife, she explained to Mr. Creach, who'd been having a pipe in the back room and so missed the transaction. Hearing what the man had paid—nearly ten times what they had paid the sailor—his eyes went round with awe, making him look more than ever like an owl. Oh, you know how it is, nothing's too good for the wife of a rich man, said Mrs. Creach, feeling a disagreeable twinge in her entrails. It eased at once, however, with her next thought, and she laughed. She'd pay that much herself, she said—just to see the look on milady's face!

"Whatever possessed you, Victor?" was Barbara's way of saying thank you. As Victor obediently bore Mitz out of her sight, she said: "By the way, I've invited the Woolves to dinner on Thursday."

15

Virginia was awake when Leonard came into her room. She had been lying in bed awake for some time, watching the sky through her window. She had heard Leonard get up and go downstairs, and she had heard Sally asking to be let out and the door opening and closing. The snow had stopped, and at this moment the sky was like cream into which a few drops of ink have been mixed. It was so still she could hear Sally panting as she labored through the snowdrifts.

As always, Leonard's first words to Virginia were: "Did you sleep well?"

Virginia nodded. "For some reason I woke up thinking of Father." (Leslie Stephen had been dead for thirty-five years.)

As Leonard put down the tray with its steaming cup of coffee, Virginia looked into his face and cried, "Mongoose!" She reached a hand out to him, and he took hold of it and said, "Come."

He led her downstairs to the dining room and showed her Mitz lying on the table. She lay encircled by her tail, the tip tucked under her chin. So Leonard had found her that morning in her cage. He had known at once, he said, when, for the first time in four and a half years, she had not come at dawn to wake him.

"We can't bury her now," he said. They would wait a day or so, until it was warmer, when Leonard would bury her near the garden wall.

They heard Sally then, asking to be let back in. She bounded into the house, wild with winter excitement, scattering snow everywhere. Leonard took her into the kitchen to chop up her breakfast, and Virginia went to drink her coffee.

They had been invited to tea with the Keyneses at their home at Tilton that day, and to dinner with Vanessa and her family at Charleston. But first, as every other morning, Leonard and Virginia went to their rooms to work.

Early that afternoon, after lunch, they pulled on their boots and went for a walk. Pink and blue shadows tinted the downs, and wild ducks circled above them.

When they returned, and before they left for Tilton, Virginia sat down and wrote a short letter to Vita, thanking her for the Strasbourg pie. She touched on a few other matters as well, and at the end of her letter she told Vita how Mitz had died: "her eyes shut and her face white like a very old womans. Leonard had taken her to sleep in his room, and she climbed onto his foot last thing."

It was Christmas Day, the last year of peace.

Acknowledgments

Although much of this unauthorized biography of Mitz has had, for want of biographical detail, to be imagined, it is based on published fact. The most important sources for Mitz's life and for information about Leonard and Virginia Woolf have been the third and fourth volumes of Leonard Woolf's autobiography, *Beginning Again* (Harvest/Harcourt Brace Jovanovich, 1975) and *Downhill All the Way* (Harvest/Harcourt Brace Jovanovich, 1975); *The Diary of Virginia Woolf,* edited by Anne Olivier Bell, assisted by Andrew McNeillie, 5 vols. (Harcourt Brace Jovanovich, 1977–84); and *The Letters of Virginia Woolf,* edited by Nigel Nicolson and Joanne Trautmann, 6 vols. (Harcourt Brace Jovanovich, 1975–80). Other works consulted include Quentin Bell's two memoirs, *Bloomsbury* (Basic Books, 1969) and *Bloomsbury Recalled* (Columbia University Press, 1996), and his *Virginia Woolf: A Biography,* 2 vols. (Harcourt Brace Jovanovich, 1972); George Spater and Ian Parsons, *A Marriage of True Minds* (Harcourt Brace Jovanovich, 1977);

and Hermione Lee, *Virginia Woolf* (Alfred A. Knopf, 1997). All quotations taken from the above sources appear in quotation marks. However, Mitz also contains dialogue that has been invented.

For information about marmosets, *Larousse Encyclopedia of Animal Life* and *Funk & Wagnalls Wildlife Encyclopedia* have been helpful.